Also By Martin Caidin

Maryjane Tonight At Angels Twelve
Cyborg

Published By
WARNER PAPERBACK LIBRARY

CYBORG #2
OPERATION NUKE

by MARTIN CAIDIN

WARNER
PAPERBACK
LIBRARY

A Warner Communications Company

WARNER PAPERBACK LIBRARY EDITION
First Printing: March, 1974

Library of Congress Catalog Card Number: 72-97689

This Warner Paperback Library Edition is published by
arrangement with Arbor House Publishing Co., Inc.

Cover art by John Mello

Warner Paperback Library is a division of Warner Books, Inc.,
75 Rockefeller Plaza, New York, N.Y. 10019.

Printed in Canada.

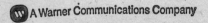 A Warner Communications Company

for Isobella
from
The Beastly Grog

CHAPTER 1

Underfoot was slime dangerous to four men struggling with a heavy, cumbersome metal case. Battery lights strapped to helmets reflected off curving wet walls. They ignored the rats, centipedes, and spiders all about them. They were stooped and bone-weary from carrying the one hundred and forty pounds of metal container along the service tunnel not quite high enough for a man to stand in. A curse as the lead man buckled to his knees.

"My ankle. I've twisted it."

Behind him a thick-bodied form lowered his end of the case to the tunnel floor. "Take a break," he said curtly. The men responded with deep, shuddering breaths, their bodies slumping.

For a moment Sam Franks was framed in light as the others cast beams from their helmet lamps on his face. Franks chewed the unlit end of a cigar. Thick fist slammed into his palm. "Just like *that* when the time comes."

The lead man rubbed his ankle. Franks unnerved him. "How much more is it now, Sam?" he asked.

Paper unfolded before a helmet light. Sam Franks studied the map, turned his light to cables with identifying numbers along the tunnel side. Finally his thick forefinger tapped the map. "We're here. Two hundred yards to go." No one spoke. Frank nodded slowly. "Let's move it," he said.

Ten feet above their heads, above concrete and macadam, spread the main square of Butukama, one of the new cities of the Congo, hacked from jungle. At one end of the

7

square loomed a government hall, standing behind huge concrete pillars. The four men were working their way to a position directly beneath the building. Inside was a meeting hall large enough to seat four hundred men, and in it were convened the new leaders of black African nations planning the best methods to remove white rule from Africa forever—to fulfill their promise for an all-black continent.

The four men in the tunnel were unconcerned with the nationalist fervor in the building above them. They were doing a job, and it was advisable to keep one's mind on the job at hand rather than on its astonishing consequences. The work also paid extraordinarily well.

The heavy metal container was put down. The men took another brief rest, then returned to work. One man went another hundred yards along the tunnel, doused his light and drew out from a shoulder holster a long-barreled pistol with a silencer. Expert fingers caressed the metal in darkness. The man was accustomed to waiting. In the other direction, another hundred yards back in the tunnel along which they had just come, another guard took his position. The remaining two men were already busy.

Sam Franks adjusted a portable fluorescent lamp, finger-punched a magnetic lock. Twelve numbers. Any one wrong number in the twelve, before depressing the "Open" key, would set off a small but devastating explosive charge. Franks didn't make that kind of error. He opened the cover and locked it into position. For several moments he took stock of the instruments and devices before him. Then he went to work adjusting a series of controls and timers. Finally he straightened, nodding. "The cable," he said, not looking up.

His assistant nodded. "Here. I've tagged it."

Franks extended a shielded wire from the container to a thick cable running the length of the tunnel. He sliced through the protective sheath to expose bare cable. To this he wound several coils of naked wire, then plugged the opposite end into a current detector. A red light stared at him. He nodded with satisfaction, removed the plug and inserted it into a receptacle in the container they had brought with them. He looked up. "Everybody on the far

8

side." He waited until the others had retraced their steps along the tunnel. He was concerned about a man slipping to dislodge the device he'd so carefully prepared. One last step. He returned his attention to another set of twelve numbered keys. For a moment he hesitated, running his tongue over dry lips. Then he bent forward, made certain of the lighting, tapped out another sequence of numbers. A series of lights glowed at him. Franks studied the color coding, nodded and closed the container. He canceled out the lock release with a final rapid movement of his fingers, turned and started after his men.

They moved quickly, silently except for the cushioned splash of boots in watery slime. No need to talk. Whatever had been accomplished so far could be undone by chance discovery. They needed to leave the area as undetected as when they'd entered Butukama. They emerged from the tunnel through a manhole cover obscured by a truck with a broken axle. Another vehicle driving by slowed and four figures slipped beneath its canvas. As the truck bounced along deeper into country with thick foliage, the men got out of their soiled clothes and put on combat jumpsuits.

The drive took the better part of an hour. Along a curving section of road the truck slowed. A radio signal beeped softly and the driver stopped. They saw no one, but the men in the truck knew they were being observed through infrared light.

"Move it." The voice came from darkness and the driver shifted gears to continue along the road, emerging at the edge of a forest clearing. At the far end a large high-winged airplane was barely visible in night shadow. The truck drove to the rear of the airplane, and this close the markings of the United States Air Force were revealed. A plane well known throughout the world—a powerful Lockheed C-130E Hercules. Made for advanced combat work. Sam Franks and the others moved into the transport while the men still spread across the field completed their final tasks. From the cockpit, Franks watched through high-powered infrared binoculars. His men knew what they were doing. Professionals. When they'd cleared the trees he wanted all signs of their presence obliterated.

Black men in Congolese uniform were brought from another truck. Hands bound tight behind their backs, short ropes holding their legs. At a signal their captors opened fire with automatic weapons. Crumpled bodies littered the side of the grass airstrip. One more prisoner, this one in the uniform of a Portuguese army captain. He was authentic, kidnapped several days before, held for this moment. One of his guards picked up a Congolese army rifle, emptied the clip into the Portuguese.

Excellent. It was assumed the blacks could be counted on to follow the example of former white exploiters. Who else had they to learn from, except the same whites they had dispossessed. But they needed things from the whites—proficiency in paramilitary activities, for example. The new nations needed more than conventional police. Quickly enough they discovered they needed real military *control*. That meant heavy firepower. It meant combining the muscle of an army with the techniques of the police.

So they would examine the bodies and discover that Portuguese bullets could only mean Portuguese guns, which meant Portuguese soldiers or at least mercenaries paid by the hated Portuguese. Who would think of an American named Sam Franks and his specialty team for hire? No way for the black Africans to connect the international organization, for which Sam Franks headed up field operations. And likewise no way for the Congolese or their colleagues to determine that antiblack, apartheid South Africa was writing the checks to finance this whole operation.

The blacks who examined the bodies of the Congolese soldiers might, of course, be suspicious. So they would cut up the body of the Portuguese officer, captured weeks before by one of Sam Franks' commando teams and kept on ice for this moment. Now his body would be found with the others, and when they investigated it they'd find Congolese bullets had killed the captain—captain of a Portuguese strike force that had gotten away, leaving him behind, its lone casualty.

The Congolese, Franks had planned, would check out the man—he *could* be a plant. They'd check him out and discover he was real enough, right down to his serial number and years of service and even his family. The

Congolese army would pass on the information to its allies. No questions any more.

The Portuguese were responsible for the slaughter. They'd be blamed for what had happened. Just as they would be blamed for what would happen tomorrow when the whole new city of Butukama disappeared.

It was all part of the contract with the "special interests" in South Africa. No fingers must be pointed. Sam Franks had understood, planned well.

By now the C-130 with U.S. Air Force markings (the U.S. was an ally of Portugal, after all, routinely helped supply her with the means of defense) was ready and the last men ran to the aircraft. The engines went to full power and with a hard forward movement the transport rushed ahead. In less than a thousand feet it was into the air and climbing steeply.

Behind the airplane timed detonators went off. At irregular intervals along the field hundred-pound explosive charges racked the night. Trucks vanished into blazing wreckage, bodies were blown in all directions, craters gouged the runway.

Sam Franks blinked as the spasms of light flashed by the climbing airplane. It would appear as planned. To the Congolese who rushed to the scene the airfield would show all the signs of a major firefight. And the craters would be evidence of a sharp, severe strike from the air.

All of which, added to the other "evidence," would make it clear the Portuguese were behind the attack and the killings. There wouldn't be enough left of the trucks to identify their source; but with all this the Congolese wouldn't need further proof. No question. Portugal must be identified as the guilty party.

If there was one thing Sam Franks liked better than a cold trail, it was a false lead.

The copilot lifted the receiver from his ear as he turned to Sam Franks. "We're cleared for straight-in."

Franks nodded. "What about the rest of it?"

"All set."

"Fine." Franks moved his seat forward and switched off the autopilot. He felt better at moments like this with

11

the big airplane responding to his hands rather than an electronic brainbox. "Tell the men," he said abruptly to the copilot, "I want full alert when we land."

Twelve minutes later the C-130 eased with squealing tires to a long macadam runway twenty miles beyond the city limits of Fort Dauphin, Malagasy, better known as Madagascar. The huge island of a quarter million square miles was ideally suited to the needs of Sam Franks and his organization. For the money Pentronics paid certain high officials they would willingly have sealed off a major part of their country. The airfield into which Franks flew the big transport was known only as K6 and had never been seen by any pilots except those of the Malagasy government and those who flew for Pentronics, Inc. In the same manner that marked his previous visits, Franks noted with satisfaction the swift efficiency of the ground crews awaiting his arrival.

The big propellers had barely stopped turning when a small army of men swarmed to the transport. Wheeled workstands surrounded the machine from nose to tail. All signs of the United States Air Force were removed. Huge letters identifying the transport with the name of British Overseas Cargo Airways appeared on the fuselage and wings. Behind the C-130, waiting to be rolled into the cabin, was a large flexible fuel tank. Fueling trucks waited to fill that tank and those in the wings as well.

Sam Franks wasted no time observing the activities about the big Lockheed. A truck drove him quickly to a wide building concealed beneath trees. Alongside the building, in its own clearing, stood a sleek twin-engined jet. Franks appraised it, then entered the building.

Inside, he accepted a mug of steaming coffee, studied the men waiting for him. A tall, slender man, Arabian, was the first to speak. "It went well, I understand."

Franks looked at him. "Not well. It went as planned."

The Arab smiled. "My apologies."

Franks sipped at the coffee. "What about payment?"

"Tonight."

"From whom?"

12

"Sperry himself. I talked with him and—"

"How did you know it was Sperry?"

"Complete voiceprint ID."

"Go on."

"They are completing transfer tonight." The Arab glanced at his watch and shrugged. "Another hour, perhaps."

"And?"

"The signal agreed upon."

Franks waited.

"I don't know." The Arab produced a sealed envelope from an inside pocket. "When the signal comes I open this. Then I know."

Franks nodded. "Good. Let me see the envelope."

The Arab returned the letter to his jacket. "Not even you."

Franks stood in front of him. "The letter, damn you, or I'll—"

"Of course." The Arab's hand emerged from his jacket with a blue-steel automatic pointed at the big man.

Franks smiled. "You're a real sorehead, Kali." He turned to another man. "What about the one-twenty-five?"

"It's ready."

Franks nodded. "All right, then, we wait for the signal. After Kali makes identification, he goes with Johnson in the one-thirty to Gibralter. Pick up the cargo there and go on to Oslo." Franks started for a door across the room. "Wake me when the signal comes in."

He was asleep seconds after he hit the couch.

The bank president blotted the signatures, placed the papers within a leather folder, and with the same unhurried sense of ceremony slid the folder into an attaché case. He leaned back in his deeply upholstered chair and smiled at the man directly across the oak conference table. For a moment he studied Jonathan Sperry, judged correctly he was of English-Irish descent. Beneath that thinning sandy hair was a hard, almost cameo-like face carved with sharp

13

edges. A wiry, hypertense, keenly intelligent man. And, thought the bank president, a very dangerous man. He shook away the feeling.

"Congratulations are certainly in order, Mr. Sperry. You know, it's not very often I stay up this late."

"It's not very often we go into the mining business," Sperry said softly.

"And diamond mining, at that. By the way, where are your mines, Mr. Sperry?"

"Another time," Sperry said. "If we are satisfied we'll have future need of your services."

The bank president murmured his pleasure. "We are honored." Who would not be honored, he thought. Eighteen million dollars worth of honor.

"Now, if you would have your secretary put through that call for me?"

"Of course, Mr. Sperry. At once, at once."

The meeting would begin in the morning. It could be the single most important event in the growth of an all-black continent. Tomorrow the final plans would be discussed. And then, at long last, the beginning of the end. Decision time was at hand. All during the day they had been arriving. Butukama was an armed camp, nothing left to chance. Every side of the conference building was guarded.

Every man was checked. Many had arrived with weapons, but they were not permitted here. The need now was for coordination, for cooperation, for a concerted plan. An Africa that would be for Africans, *real* Africans.

Black Africa had waited two years for this moment. For the first time an all-black Congress would emerge, and after that, the continent would return to rightful rule.

They watched the Arab, Kali, as he brought the receiver to his ear, listened intently, then placed the telephone between his ear and his shoulder, freeing both hands. He tore open the envelope he took from his jacket and unfolded the paper.

"Again, please," he said into the phone. "All right," he said after a lengthy pause. He replaced the phone on its cradle and motioned to another man.

14

"Wake him," he directed. The man went into the room where Sam Franks slept.

Franks was there at once, no sign of sleep in his heavy face, his eyes intent on Kali.

Kali gestured with the paper. "Confirmation," he smiled.

Franks nodded. "And the meeting?"

"That also is confirmed," replied the Arab. "They are almost ready. The full session is scheduled to take place at nine in the morning. Congo time. One last group is arriving in the morning. They should all be together by ten at the very latest. That is the time recommended for—"

Franks gestured and the Arab was silent, waiting.

"Did you speak with John personally?" Franks asked.

"With Mr. Sperry himself."

"No doubts?"

"None."

Franks was dealing in a payment of eighteen million dollars for a nuke, and his special services for its deployment and guaranteed effective use. He believed it appropriate, under the circumstances, to ask questions even if he knew the answers ahead of time. It helped expel nagging doubts. Franks turned suddenly to a heavily armed man in a flight suit.

"Okay. We go for wheels up at six-thirty sharp."

CHAPTER 2

He sat immobile, a hulking Buddha, halfway around the world from Sam Franks, but already linked to him in a way neither man could be aware of. Jackson McKay looked at the report on his desk, then shook his head, a slow gesture that said a great deal to the man seated across his desk.

Oscar Goldman watched the director of the Office of Special Operations with customary fascination. Thirty years of intelligence and espionage work. An efficient killer with his hands or any weapon at his disposal. A veteran of British Intelligence and Interpol. One of the men who made up the hard core of the World War II Office of Strategic Services. From OSS to CIA, and then this new organization, OSO—Office of Special Operations; specialist *non pareil* to all other security and intelligence organizations. McKay was one of the few men in the Washington intelligence hierarchy who was not soundly cursed by those he worked with.

And Oscar Goldman was his right hand, alter ego. Goldman no more looked his part than the corpulent McKay did his. Goldman was an unimposing figure at seven inches less than six feet, but his apprenticeship had been served as a special-agent paratrooper and ranger. McKay believed Goldman was a genius in sizing up people, converting them to service for OSO. He was also a man with an extraordinary grasp of weapons technology. He held that rare distinction of being able to correlate an enormous quantity of facts from various disciplines.

Goldman was also responsible for Steve Austin. Not the Colonel Steve Austin known to the world as test pilot and commander of Apollo 17, the last manned flight to the moon. In fact, not an ordinary man at all.

There was a Steve Austin the outside world knew nothing about.

Cyborg. A man who was humanly vulnerable yet more than a man, an exquisite blending of shattered body, biological engineering and electronics—a new cybernetic organism.

The man they looked upon as the first cyborg had proven an extraordinary new element of OSO, and McKay thought of him now as he looked at the report on his desk, and considered a mission that—again unknown to any of them—would link Austin with the fortunes of Sam Franks and world forces only forming at the time. McKay had not

16

been present that morning Austin had sailed an incredible swooping curve back from the thin edges of space in a nasty metal beast they called the M3F5—prelude to giant space shuttles to come. The morning when the wicked little machine slammed into the hard, dry desert floor of California, ripped across the desert disintegrating, mangling a helpless Steve Austin. One moment superb test pilot, astronaut, human being of special talent and intelligence.

The next, when the shattered wreckage ground to a stop in the desert, there was no man inside. Instead the rescue crew removed a battered, crushed, torn, and lacerated thing—mercifully unconscious. The rescue team was good, the medical team incredible. And one doctor above all the others. Rudy Wells, bearded, moving through medicine and beyond; the only man who could venture, through his love and empathy, into the terror of Austin's mind.

The list ran through McKay's thoughts: both legs amputated. The left arm mangled, torn from the body. Ribs shattered, jaw smashed; replaced with metal alloys and plastics and ceramics. Beautiful open heart surgery and implantation of a Hufnagel valve. There was more: blinded in his left eye. Skull fracture. Concussion.

The surgeons, especially two named Ashburn and Killian, kept the body alive. Rudy Wells attended to the mind and spirit of Steve Austin, subjecting himself willingly (because it was necessary) to Austin's abuse.

And Steve Austin survived. Precariously, but he survived. Wells kept him unconscious for weeks. Time was the friend now. Time for the shock to dissipate from the system, for trillions of cells to reform and to adjust to whatever life decreed for their intelligence of new inner creation. And then that was past.

The bionics laboratory was carved deep into the flanks of the Colorado Rockies. When OSO director McKay learned what had happened to a man named Steve Austin, he immediately dispatched Oscar Goldman. The bionics laboratory was engineering and life sciences and cybernetics and biology wrapped up into a single gleaming package. There were men there who knew how to run through a giant computer every element of construction and move-

17

ment of, for example, the human arm and hand. The computer digested what it learned, but so extraordinary was the creation of flesh and blood, sinew and tendon and muscle, veins and arteries and nerves, of bone and marrow and pulsing liquid flow, of trillions of cells, that the computer taxed even its own capabilities in reducing to intelligible numbers the handwork of God. The numbers finally were translated to digits with special meaning to eagerly waiting scientists and doctors and technicians. In those mathematical symbols they found the blueprints for creating a living simulation, fashioned from artificial materials, of what had been a human arm. Or leg, or elbow, or rib, or knee, or finger. It could all be reduced to digital form and from that form could be recreated a living entity.

Some argued the semantics of "living." The human body functions on messages carried through electrical impulses generated by electro-chemical reaction. Nervous energy is electrical energy, even if the wonderful intricacy of the human form seems to deserve a better analogy than to a weak self-powered battery.

Bionics did not contest the semantics. Nor did it solicit agreement. Their creed, under the direction of Dr. Michael Killian, was the work itself. Bionics. *Bios* from the Greek for life, and *ics* to represent in the manner after. A bionics limb was a recreation of a living member, and Steve Austin—cyborg—functioned in a manner as unusual as the concept from which he emerged.

His heart valves were damaged? Replace them with the Hufnagel valve and supporting internal apparatus. His skull was crushed? Replace the bone with cesium and with new alloys where needed. Design a spongy center layer and another outer layer to protect the brain case inside. He could then endure a direct blow ten times greater—without suffering injury—than the sledgehammer thuds that cracked his skull in the first place.

Replace ribs. Install—and *install* was the proper word—added tendons, plastic valves, arteries and veins where needed.

Blinded in his left eye? Well, they weren't *that* good. Not Dr. Killian, nor Dr. Wells, nor anyone else, because the human eye is a miracle of jelly and water and light-

18

sensitive elements and rods and electrical impulses trickling their way through bundles of nerves to a gray convoluted mass of three pounds encased within the skull—no, they couldn't yet restore vision when the optic nerve was mangled, and Austin's optical nerve was so much biological garbage. But they could make use of the area where there had been an eyeball to build a marvelously small and efficient camera into where his living camera system had been. Steve Austin became a man with one living eye and one extraordinary camera that recorded on tiny super-sensitive film what its human carrier saw with the living eye.

None of these could compare with the miracle of the re-created living limbs—to the arm with its elbow and its bionics bones and cartilage and the never-believed dexterity of wrist and fingers and opposed digit, as well as the legs with their computer-directed systems.

It was one thing to construct the limbs that were to receive the nerve impulses flowing to and from the brain, nerve impulses that were electrical signals. It was another to mimic the nerve fibers and systems for transmitting the impulses from the brain into the spinal cord and on down the message networks. To Steve Austin's arm stump they double-engaged the bionics and the natural bone to exceed by far the original level of strength and resistance. They connected actual nerves and muscles with bionics nerves and muscles. But the signals that came through, while they well served natural flesh and its constituent elements, were hopelessly weak for a bionics system. So within the arm and the legs went small nuclear-powered generators that spun silently at speeds measured in thousands of revolutions per second.

The signal flashed through Steve Austin until it reached part of him that was living by computer and machine lathe, where it was sensed and flashed to an amplifier. Now it was retransmitted at many times greater strength than when received. The small nuclear generators fed power through the artificial duplications of nature's pulleys and cables, which moved, twisted, pulled, bent, contracted, squeezed. But artificial fingertips tended to be insensitive, and a cybernetic hand could crush human bone with no more effort than was needed to pulp a rose. So they added vibrating pads, sensors, amplifiers, feedback. Now the steel-boned hand that could kill with a single transmitted impulse could also lovingly caress a lover's skin.

For months Steve Austin, reborn as cyborg, went through hell to create a physical and emotional knowledge and acceptance of himself. For months he stumbled and fell, weaved and swayed; his systems jerked spasmodically, they shorted and surged; he was clumsy, crude, full of rage. But finally, with the devoted help of a giant of a man—in size and heart—by the name of Marty Schiller, a man with two artificial limbs, Steve Austin made it, and learned there *were* compensations.

If the bionics arm was not quite the same as the original limb, it was in many ways superior. The same for the legs. Steve Austin's arm was more than a human arm; it was also capable of performing as a battering ram, a vise, a bludgeon—a tool and a weapon. His legs were also tremendous pistons. His heart and circulatory systems served a body without the need of supporting two legs and an arm. The bionics systems with their nuclear amplifiers attended to all energy needs, and so Austin's endurance increased dramatically. He was dependent as ever on his heart and lungs and other systems. But he could run a day and a night because there was no energy drain from the legs hammering against the earth.

But what of the psychology of a man who had suffered impotence—not through genital injury or damage to the nerve network splicing the spinal column. No, through fear that no woman could feel or make love to a creature half-man and half-machine.

That too had been overcome; not scientifically but by the oldest, most effective potion—the love of a good woman. Austin survived his crises, but he was still a man, and whatever superior powers he now enjoyed were still subject to the many ways he was vulnerable. A bullet through the heart would kill him. He could drown, suffocate, be poisoned, or crushed.

His defenses did soar in efficiency, his reactions swifter than the most skilled athlete's. His body made him potentially a killing mechanism, especially when integrated with miniaturized weaponry in his bionics arm and legs.

Jackson McKay had authorized twelve million dollars to Project Cyborg, and it had already paid off in two assignments so far: A mission into a secret Soviet submarine base on the northeast coast of South America, on which Austin learned information that later brought about the end of that base. And a mission into Egypt against Soviet-sponsored Arab extremists, for which he needed the skill of a pilot, acquired many years before, plus the extraordinary endurance of the cyborg. Again a critical threat had been eliminated, although the toll on Steve Austin—as man and cyborg—had been considerable.

Men heal, cyborgs don't, but they can be repaired, rebuilt, even improved. Austin had been back at the secret bionics laboratory in Colorado for several months now. The rejuvenation process was finished. Whatever he had been before he was more now, if for no other reason than the experience as a cyborg he'd had time to acquire.

We need him again, McKay thought as he glanced at the papers on his desk. Steve Austin was surely their best chance against the threatening events described in the report before him.

The problem, as usual, had been dumped in OSO's lap. CIA had burned its fingers; State was fluttering its hands in the fashion McKay had come to detest; and the military were honing their knives for a super-commando firefight. None of them, McKay felt certain, even remotely approached a solution to the problem.

McKay's priority signal light flashed on his desk. He pressed the button that would pick up his voice from anywhere in the room. "Go ahead."

"Colonel Austin is here, sir," a secretary said.

McKay glanced at Goldman. "Send him in."

The door slid noiselessly to one side and Steve Austin stepped through. The door closed immediately. For the moment Austin stood quietly, only his eyes moving. Eye, singular, Goldman corrected himself. He looked at the ex-fighter pilot, six feet one inch tall, flat-bellied and wide-shouldered on a lean-muscled frame. An aura of confidence, blue eyes. Eye, the left one is plastic, Goldman again reminded himself. Those incredible bionic limbs . . .

21

He should have weighed 180 pounds. He didn't. He weighed nearly 240 because of the metal and the other systems, but he carried it all with ease. No, not quite, thought Goldman. He carries it with the indifference of any man who knows what he is.

McKay rose ponderously to his feet, in itself extraordinary. McKay preferred the pull of gravity holding him to his seat. "Good to see you," McKay said. Austin, with the fluid movement they'd learned to expect from him, slid into the one empty seat before the desk.

Jackson McKay made a steeple of his thick fingers and peered over them at Steve Austin.

"Do you know, for example, how to set off an atomic bomb?"

"I do, and you knew the answer to the question before you asked it. So why ask?"

"Because," said McKay, "we may want you to steal an atom bomb. Defuse it. Or perhaps even set it off, as well."

CHAPTER 3

Steve Austin leaned back in his chair and crossed his legs, a reflex of his constant desire to at least appear ordinary whenever possible.

"Any bomb in particular?" he asked in answer to McKay's remarkable statement.

"It's difficult to say. At the moment, anyway, but—"

"It could also be a thermonuclear bomb," Oscar Goldman added.

"If you don't mind, please spell it out," Austin told McKay.

McKay did, but in his own fashion. "You once commanded a strike force of FB-111 fighter-bombers. You operated from secret fields in Canada and Alaska. You were required to be familiar with the weapons accommodated by your aircraft."

Austin held up his right hand with three fingers extended, not pleased with the memory. "Three thermonukes per airplane, each equal to twelve million tons of TNT."

"And the mechanisms?" McKay said quietly.

"It was a long time ago."

"But not so long that you've forgotten."

Steve looked at the OSO director. "It's in the past. Finished. Are you suggesting I get back into *that* business?"

"I suggest you get back into the nuclear weapons business. Look, I expect you, as much as any sane man, to have automatic revulsion against nuclear weapons. I also expect you know who and what I am, what this organization does, and you know that throwing bombs around is hardly the sort of thing we're up to."

For the first time Steve Austin evaded the eyes of the heavy man behind the desk. McKay did not miss the movement. "By the way, something happened to you even before your crash, didn't it? Something that changed you inside as much as the crash smashed you up physically."

"There are times, McKay," Steve said, "when you really surprise me. You're right. It happened out there, coming around the moon. The very first time, I mean. The effect was greatest then. And every time we had a chance to look at the earth after that, when we took the time to *really* look, to try to understand what we were seeing, well, it's overwhelming. You come around this dead, cratered world and suddenly over the horizon, a quarter of a million miles away, it's there. Home. That's how you think of it. Like the word never had meaning before. It rolls through space, this beautiful blue world floating against the blackest black there ever was, and you feel you could look around the other side of the earth. The pictures, the films, they don't mean anything because they're flat. But you see it as a round ball, and you hold up both hands by the window of the spacecraft, and you can cup the world in your hands and . . . and well, all of a sudden you feel how fragile it is . . . Anyway, maybe you can at least understand why I can't ever have anything to do with weapons that could tear apart what I saw from out there. Do you understand?"

"I think so," McKay said quietly, "and that's why, more now than ever before, it's vital to you to be involved again with nukes."

Steve stared at McKay, disbelief in his eyes.

"We need you to help *stop* bombs from going off."

"But you said something before about my stealing an atom bomb, even a thermonuke and—"

"And maybe even setting it off," McKay finished for him. "Look, if you have a situation where you know a bomb is intended to go off in a city, and you can get your hands on that particular weapon and there's no way to keep it from going off, then isn't it better to detonate the thing when it's *not* in the city?"

"That's a hell of a lot of supposing. And who am I supposed to steal this nuke from?"

"We don't know that yet," McKay said.

"Let me really spell it out for you. We're talking about an international black market in nuclear weapons," Goldman said, "that can make possible the ultimate blackmail —and maybe worse."

"You're kidding."

Goldman shook his head. "I wish we were. We've been working on this for a long time . . . this organization and nearly every security and intelligence outfit in the world, including the Russians, Interpol, our allies and theirs. We work with anybody we can because each of us has known that sooner or later one or more nukes would get into the hands of criminals—meaning anyone who gets involved with nuclear weapons to meet a political or nationalistic goal."

"Or," McKay's voice came from behind his desk, "for cash."

"You are telling me," Steve said slowly, "that people have somehow managed to get their hands on nuclear devices and have put them up *for sale?*"

"Precisely," McKay said. "Not to mention their special delivery services."

"That's hard to believe," Steve told him.

"Why?" demanded Goldman.

"For one thing, the system of controls, of monitoring. It—"

"Isn't foolproof, by any means," Goldman broke in. "Forgive me, Steve, but I'm afraid a crash course in reality is in order."

"Go ahead," Steve said, feeling a sudden weariness from the foreknowledge that he was going to be led into something he liked less with each of Goldman's words.

"Right now the United States has in its inventory something like fifty thousand atomic weapons of all kinds," Goldman continued. "That's every type of warhead you can think of, from the big hydrogen bombs we carry in our planes to the smallest weapons for battlefield use. Warheads for air-to-air missiles, for artillery, for battlefield missiles. Thousands of these are small, efficient, and powerful. You said yourself that one FB-111 could carry three thermonukes with a total yield of thirty-six million tons of TNT. Okay, and the smaller weapons have anywhere from a kiloton on up. The key here is that we're talking about nukes that are small in physical size. Some of these things could fit into a cookie jar.

"Now think about where these nukes go. They're all over the world. They're stored at various military bases. When you have that many nukes in so many places, you tend to become vulnerable in your security, and sooner or later you lose some. How many have been lost at sea because of planes going down from engine trouble or some other reason? And how many of those bombs were recovered *without our knowing about it?* Take a big army base somewhere in Europe, nuclear warheads on the premises. The outfit moves, or there's a fire, records lost, destroyed or stolen, and in the end no one is absolutely sure some of these weapons aren't missing."

"Not *sure?* About nukes? That I still find hard to believe."

"Believe it. And even if we didn't face the problem of numbers, we *know* about certain weapons being stolen. We know of raids by persons or groups unknown against certain storage areas. And then there's the problem of a

25

few of our own people defecting, and taking one or more bombs with them. It isn't that hard, Steve, when a man can put a warhead into an attaché case and desert. If he can sell that nuke, he'd have enough money to change his name and appearance and buy his way to a life of luxury. *It's happened, Steve.* Not only to us but to the Russians. We said before we've been working closely with them because we're equally vulnerable."

"It's another reason," McKay broke in, "why the explosion of one or even more atomic bombs would no longer precipitate a war between the major powers. We know and they know, and this includes most governments, that there's more than a few of these things around. It's strange, but in a way the knowledge that there have been losses of these weapons to the black market has helped prevent atomic war between the major powers. Someone might threaten to set off a nuclear blast in even a major city and it wouldn't automatically—as in the early post-World War II days—be assumed it was a hostile government; the ultimate blackmail could also be in the hands of these international gangsters. That's why our people in Washington, their people in Moscow, London, Paris, and elsewhere, have at least tacitly agreed that no one reacts automatically any more."

Steve shook his head slowly. "The idea of losing actual warheads seemed far-fetched to me. But I've got to admit that even if bombs weren't missing, it's possible for trained people to make their own bombs. Breeder reactors produce fissionable material as a waste product from turning out electricity. You can take this waste product and make your own bombs. And they make a special problem all their own."

Now McKay looked confused.

"Anything you in effect build at home," Steve went on, "has got to be a radioactively dirty bomb.

"A couple of us, in fact, *built* our own atomic bomb as part of a research project, and it wasn't that big a deal. Take the breeder reactor I mentioned. You use the breeder to produce commercial electricity. The last time we looked at the figures there were some five hundred reactors already built or under construction in something like

26

seventy different countries. They have differences in design, of course, but they all work on the same principle. You burn natural or slightly enriched uranium in the reactor, it produces tremendous heat, the heat is cycled through a closed loop system to produce electricity. But as you burn the uranium fuel you're modifying it, and what comes out as a waste product is plutonium. Once you have the basic material, the plutonium, the rest is pretty much a matter of mechanical and electrical hardware. Six kilograms of plutonium and a machine shop and you're in business."

"My God," McKay said. "You mean it takes only fourteen pounds of the stuff to—"

"That's for an inefficient, clumsy, homegrown bomb," Steve said.

"Let's hear more about how you made yours," McKay said.

"We didn't use actual plutonium. No need to be *that* realistic, not at first, anyway. There are two types of bombs you can build. The shotgun—which is what we used at Hiroshima—and the implosion weapon, which we used at Nagasaki and is far more complicated in its design and construction. With the right materials, any good machine shop or laboratory can build either weapon, but we stuck with the easy one. The basic idea is to separate your main pieces of plutonium. The optimum shape is a sphere. We worked with lead, but it adds up the same. We cut the lead sphere so that one shape was a wedge, and the other, or receiving end, had an indentation of exactly the right size to receive the wedge. When you brought them together they formed a sphere. The trick is to keep the two pieces apart so they won't form a critical mass."

"Which is?" McKay said.

"In pure form, anything over twelve pounds."

"And if you have critical mass, as you call it—"

"More properly called the K-factor," Steve said.

"And if you bring together your plutonium to form a critical mass, what happens?"

"You get yourself an atomic bomb. The plutonium is always undergoing *some* fission. But since it's not in a critical mass, the neutrons escape and there's no danger. But

27

if you get two subcritical masses near each other, the fission rate goes up, you get tremendous heat and radiation. The whole mechanism would melt before you could ever get the bomb. So you bring the two slugs together as fast as possible and keep them there for a fraction of a second before the whole thing blows apart.

"We used a machine shop to build a grooved barrel. The plutonium slugs were at each end, fitted to rods that in turn fitted to the grooves. We built a ripple-fire series of explosive charges at the end of the barrel that contained the wedge. Then, for good measure, we added a small rocket motor that fired a fraction of a second after the explosive charges were set to go off. It was triple redundancy to assure that the whole mess would come together. The rocket was added insurance if the explosives didn't work as intended."

"What about the materials for the mechanism?" McKay asked. "Where did you get those?"

"Hardware stores, mainly."

"Stock items?"

"Stock items. What hardware didn't carry, we got in special machine shops. Remember, they build things for cars, airplanes, skin divers, and anybody else who comes along. No way to figure a bomb was being built."

"How did you set it off?"

"Radio signal detonator as primary. Time-signal charge as backup."

"Any special problems?"

"Yes," Steve said. "Plutonium is corrosive. The surface comes apart quickly. So we built in humidity and temperature control. In fact, the bomb was the easiest part. The auxiliary equipment took the most time and trouble."

"The weight?"

"We surprised ourselves," Steve said. "Nine hundred and forty-six pounds on the nose. Not bad, when you consider the Hiroshima bomb weighed *ten thousand pounds*. But we didn't have to drop ours from a plane, we didn't bother with the barometric pressure or impact detonators and the other systems they used for the air drop."

"How big?"

"Four feet long by seventeen inches wide."

"I thought," McKay said, "your bomb was a dummy only. Now you imply it worked."

"It did. The weapons lab people were running a more realistic test than we knew. They took our bomb, substituted plutonium for the lead we used, stuck it in a hole in the test grounds, and set it off."

From McKay, "And?"

"Twenty-two thousand tons of explosion."

Through dinner in McKay's office Steve argued that his personal experience with nuclear weapons was hardly unique, that there were plenty of people who knew more and had done more, including "people who assemble them, work on their design, tear down and service them." Except none of these people had his special qualities and training, and the very fact of the loose situation in the control of nukes, feasibility of stealing or even fashioning them from obtainable fissionable materials and hardware all made plausible the concept of an organization that exploited this situation. But the way McKay and Goldman now developed it with Steve it became much more than a concept.

"Suppose you've been able to create a strong international organization whose intent is criminal and whose facade is respectable. We're talking about millions of dollars worth of equipment, facilities, organization."

"So you don't bother robbing banks," Steve said.

McKay nodded. "You go for bigger game. You have one item to sell that could justify your tremendous investment. But having something that expensive to sell restricts the range of potential customers. A government, for example. One political group trying to overthrow another. Let's say your item is a nuclear device. You also offer for hire your services in providing such devices where and when needed."

"Which means you may not ever set them off," Steve said slowly. "Because if you can convince the other guy you have the nukes where you say they are, and can detonate them when you want to. . . ."

"Except you must be prepared to prove your point,"

29

McKay added. "The best bluff is one you've proved you can back up if necessary. Now, given the organization and what it does, including dealing in nuclear devices, would you use the so-called basement bomb for your business?"

Steve thought about that. Any such organization, to operate successsfully, would need freedom of movement, which meant not being tied down to cumbersome procedures or equipment. And the so-called basement bomb was clumsy, oversized, and very heavy. Okay if you were trying to start a revolution on a one-shot basis, but not for long-range planning by the international organization described by McKay.

"If you build your own bomb," Steve said, "you've got a whole bagful of problems. First, you're going to have to move the thing. That involves shock absorbers and the equipment to monitor the internal systems of the device. And that in turn adds to the complexity of a portable power source for just this one purpose, even if you're using batteries you throw away. The point is that with any crude device the problems of having the thing ready for immediate use are huge.

"Also, if it's the kind of package you build with a home workshop or even with a professional shop—we're talking about something less than a really pro weapons lab— you're never going to get the kind of seals you need for effective humidity and temperature control. And you need that kind of sealed control, because temperature changes can cause metal to shrink or expand, and the same goes for plastics or other materials, and you can end up with a hell of an expensive dud. So again you end up needing a portable power source to handle such problems.

"This is why that first bomb, the one we used in Japan, was so damned big and cumbersome. Another problem in mobility is your external casing. Do you want to drop the thing from a plane? Or do you want to get it into a harbor with a ship? And the more complicated you get, the more I suppose you risk exposure. Let's say you want to set the thing off from a distance. Is it electrical? Do you tie in to a local power source? Maybe you drag it into a city with a truck. But it's too dangerous to leave it there, so you move it from the truck to an apartment, or a store. You've got to be sure it's well hidden, and you'll need antennas and all kinds of radio gear to get the right signal to set it off—if it's a radio signal you want to use, which is the safest way. And all these things mean weight, complexity, cumbersome gear on your hands. It's got to be at best a one-shot effort."

"He's right," Goldman said. "You could get away with this maybe once or twice, but not much more."

"Well, even if they aren't caught right away," Steve added, "it wouldn't be hard to track them down. Any time you set off a basement nuke you've got a dirty bomb. Dirty in radioactivity. Any cloud from the bomb has traces of the original materials, and you know the experts can break down those traces and give you damn near everything but the fingerprints of the people who put the thing together."

"What if it's a professional weapon?" McKay asked.

"You can still trace the elements from sampling the radioactive cloud," Steve said, "but it might not do much good. I assume you'd be dealing with smart professionals who knew what they were about. The bomb they'd use could be easily transported in a sealed system. The only maintenance to worry about would be taken care of in some secret or disguised facility that was fully equipped."

"How long can you work with one of these sealed units without maintenance?"

"I guess with the smaller bombs you could go months without much trouble."

"Smaller bombs?" McKay's eyes were intense.

Steve was reluctant to say it. "You can carry a one-point-one megatonner in a large attaché case."

"One million tons in an attaché case?"

"One million one hundred thousand tons yield. We've had them for years."

"What about a really *small* bomb?"

"A hundred kiloton bomb—five times more powerful than the bomb we used at Hiroshima—is about the size of a kitchen toaster."

"Well," McKay said. "We definitely are in trouble, because those are the weapons that appear to be up for sale. And from what we've been able to learn so far a service goes along with purchase of the weapon."

"You've got proof of this?"

"Proof is for juries. You decide for yourself." McKay reached into a desk drawer and tossed a thick document onto the desk. "This is a collection of intelligence reports from every security agency in the country. Some of them you've never heard of. Also from Russian agencies. They all point convincingly to an international group dealing in stolen nuclear weapons.

"But, like you say, it's not *proof*," McKay added, "and we go just so far by conventional investigation and even less far in effective follow-up—without concrete, on-the-spot evidence. We're pretty much convinced that there's an organization that operates internationally or that's been set up for some time and is about to begin operation any minute. And not only with nuclear weapons. Apparently they offer complete paramilitary services to paying customers."

Goldman added, "They've got a superb organization. So good we haven't been able to learn much more than that they exist. They're so powerful that certain governments are willing to provide complete seclusion and anonymity for them in return for pay and special protection."

"What about the CIA?" Steve asked.

"They've lost fourteen people to date," McKay said.

"Fourteen experienced people," Goldman added. "Perhaps a hundred more local agents in different parts of the world. Military intelligence has lost another twenty or thirty. As you can see, sending out agents to nail down the information we want doesn't seem to work very well."

Steve sighed. "All right, let's hear it."

Goldman began: "You're the best chance we have. With your special talents, especially your background as a pilot and as someone who's worked with nuclear weapons you—"

"I get the picture, Oscar."

"We want you to infiltrate this organization. You're known all over the world as the man who commanded the last flight to the moon."

"Which would set me up, I should think, as the perfect target."

"We've worked it out," McKay broke in. "Look, you know what's at stake. You know why you've got the best chance to do what the others couldn't. And if that isn't enough, then I suggest you remind yourself what you just told us about looking at this blue planet earth from a quarter of a million miles away, and what atomic bombs can and will do to it."

Steve Austin had no answer to that. It was a case of eating his own words.

CHAPTER 4

At the hidden airfield twenty miles beyond Fort Dauphin on Malagasy, everything was ready. Sam Franks had said wheels up at six-thirty *sharp*. Five minutes before deadline the swept-wing jet was at the runway, engines idling, all clean and ready in the cockpit. For this flight Franks would fly as copilot in the right seat. He preferred the man at his left to be concerned with the exact distance for take-off calculated in terms of weight, temperature, density, altitude.

Nothing was left to chance. The winds aloft at succeeding levels of 3,000 feet were known all the way to 45,000 feet, above which there were no standard reports. No matter; they'd determine that information from their on-board inertial computer system as they climbed. The pilot in the left seat, had he not been thoroughly familiar with Sam Franks as a pilot, would never have known that every detail had been checked out and evaluated by Franks. No wonder. It hadn't been that many years since Franks had flown B-52 and B-58 bombers for the Strategic Air Command. Any man once singled out by General Curtis LeMay as the top bomber jock in SAC had to be in a class all his own. Those who flew with or for Sam Franks did so with a fine cutting edge.

Thirty seconds before six-thirty the de Havilland DH-125 rolled out onto the runway, pointed directly down the long strip. The brakes locked. With five seconds to go the engines screamed at takeoff power. Exactly at six-thirty the pilot chopped the brakes free and the airplane surged forward, accelerating with a thundering rush. On each side of the runway, cut from heavy forest, thousands of birds took to the air with frightened cries, casting mottled shadows through the sun still low on the horizon. And then the plane was gone, leaving behind a thin booming cry drifting away like final ripples on a lake.

Within the jet there was little sound. The pilot eased control from his hands to the automatic pilot, coupled to the inertial computer. Everything had been preset, fed carefully into the electronic innards of the compact robot brain. As the machine surged steadily into the morning skies the computer compared its predicted passage over the slow slide of distant horizon. Cape Sainte-Marie to wind at different heights flashed on a digital readout panel. Compensation was automatic, and it was the human pilot who scribbled notes on a kneepad, leaving the robot to tend to its ministrations.

They seemed a sealed spore drifting higher and higher with no apparent effort. No real sense of motion beyond the slow slide of distant horizon. Cape Sainte-Marie to their left was visible only briefly. Their steep angle of climb and breathless rush into thinning air swept it quickly from view. The jet angled smoothly to the northwest, climbing constantly as it crossed the Mozambique Channel. Just north of Nampula it edged over the continent proper. Several moments later the altimeter circled around to a reading of 25,000 feet. Now, for the first time since he activated the autopilot, the man in the left seat returned to direct control of the machine.

This was no ordinary DH-125, although it would have

34

taken an expert observer to detect the wings were nine feet wider than the standard airplane's; at high altitudes they performed with the lifting characteristics of a high-speed glider. Close study would show an inlet for each engine at least fourteen inches wider than the power plants normally fitted to the de Havilland. They could not be advanced to full power until they reached five miles above the earth for fear of structural failure. Now, with a steady and careful movement, the pilot rested his right hand on the throttles, edged them forward, watching his fuel flow and pressure gauges. Then they were full forward. The DH-125 climbed with a fighter's speed and rate of ascent.

Tabora in Tanganyika, due south of Lake Victoria, lay directly beneath the airplane as they eased into level flight at 68,000 feet. The great height banished all sense of motion. The distant horizon of the planet itself curved visibly before them. It was an extraordinary moment, the air above a dark, almost-purple blue, the rounded edge of earth mantled with a sun-slashed silver haze.

Sam Franks paid it no attention. He had left the cockpit to another man. Now he sat hunched before a large instrument panel. On a grid map illuminated beneath a plexiglass sheet, the terrain far below moved slowly on rollers, and a bright dot represented their exact position. Kigoma would be just north of their position as they flew due west. Franks felt the slight turn. The winds were stronger than expected and the robot brain was compensating. Within minutes they would cross the Congo River, and shortly after they would be 110 miles due north of Butukama, where several hundred men argued the future of an all-black continent.

In the high-columned meeting hall at the center of Butukama the meeting had come to a violent halt. Delegates of every black government and secret conclave were on their feet, their faces distorted with shouted anger. Fists were shaken in the air as the conference hall rocked with curses and cries for blood. *Not* for whites. Not at this moment, anyway.

All eyes followed several black men in chains dragged onto the main floor. The delegates, seated in ascending, staggered rows as within an indoor arena, looked down on the captives kept to the floor beneath rifle butts and booted feet. Then a momentary interruption as another group was dragged, already dead, and placed against one wall.

Colonel Jomo Mwanza, chief of the special security force to protect the gathering, stood in the center of the hall, arms upraised in a sudden gesture for silence. It came quickly. Mwanza turned slowly, his face gleaming from the rain, and looked up at the faces of the assembly. Finally, achieving his intended effect, he turned to point to the figures on the floor.

"Look at them," he said. "They are traitors, hired by the Portuguese to sabotage us. They are responsible for the deaths of our own brothers last night. Some, as you can see, we managed to capture alive. It will be a pleasure to see them regret it."

The president of the assembly leaned forward. "It is only a few hours since the treacherous attack last night, and we already have the evidence that the Portuguese have never given up their old colonial ways. And, worse, some of our own people have yet to learn that we mean to take back this continent. Their skins may be black. But they have hearts that are white. They are worse than the whites."

He rose slowly, and ordered Colonel Mwanza to execute them, with the Assembly as silent witness.

Thirteen miles above the earth the jet with its rakishly swept-back wings drifted across the continent. Sam Franks sat with eyes fixed on the instruments in front of him. Finally he reached forward with his right hand, snapped back a protective cover to reveal a wide, red button.

They crossed an invisible line from Stanleyville in the north running due south until it reached Butukama. This was the line of decision. Of commitment. Sam Franks waited. The fourth man aboard the airplane nodded. "Sixty seconds."

"Open the safety locks."

"Safety locks open. Thirty seconds."

"Call them off," Franks said.

The sound of machine guns violated the meeting hall. It was over quickly. The roar echoed through the high chamber, and the stench of gunpowder drifted up to the delegates.

Colonel Mwanza then walked forward slowly, unholstering the .38 at his right side. He stood before the first body, bringing his gun slowly forward. His thumb brought back the hammer with a click heard by each of the hundreds of men in the room. He pointed the gun at the head of the first man. His finger tightened, squeezing slowly. The hammer released, only an instant away from detonating the round in the chamber.

Only an instant.

It never came.

"Ten seconds, Sam."

"Confirm safety locks open."

"Confirmed."

"Count."

"Five seconds.

"Four.

"Three.

"Two.

"One."

Sam Franks pressed the red button.

In less time than it took for the hammer in the gun held by Colonel Jomo Mwanza to travel from its cocked position to strike the bullet, the radio signal flashed out from the jet thirteen miles above the earth, more than a hundred miles north of Butukama, where it fed into a high television tower and sped through the coaxial cable in the service tunnel beneath the conference building to the wire spliced into the cable hours before by Sam Franks.

The heavy container left in the tunnel enclosed a series of concentric spheres, of which the outermost was plastic. This surrounded a sphere of plutonium, which in turn encircled a sphere of beryllium. Gold-plated cones lay in the center of the beryllium. Surrounding the set of multiple spheres was a system of thirty-eight lenses, each made up of a plastic explosive, each wired to two detonators. Each detonator was wired to a condenser, so that the radio signal flashed from the DH-125 jet and translated to an electrical signal would bring each of the explosive lenses to detonate at the same instant.

The signal flashed to the condensers, to the detonators, to the lenses, which vanished. They did not explode. They *imploded,* the terrible explosive pressure rammed inward against the porous plutonium sphere. The vanishing explosive lenses became a single concave shock wave front all about the surface of the plutonium sphere. Instantly the plutonium was compressed into a hypercritical mass. The beryllium core also collapsed. The gold-plated cones no longer restricted a flow of neutrons. The plutonium mass was critical—the K-factor. And because of the neutron activity the mass destroyed itself.

The mechanical process of electrical activity through the system of condensers, detonators, and imploding lenses took barely a thousandth of a second. It was at this moment that Colonel Jomo Mwanza's squeezing finger released the cocked hammer of his revolver. At the moment the hammer cracked against the bullet the mechanical process in the service tunnel beneath the building ended. At that millionth of a second when the spherical object in the service tunnel ceased to exist, a small star was born.

Directly beneath the building where the leaders of the new Africa were meeting, where bodies lay collapsed against the marble floor, where hundreds of men watched in silence as Colonel Mwanza squeezed a trigger, a *thing* with a temperature of sixty million degrees came into being.

In that moment the service tunnel, the ground beneath, the soil in all directions for a thousand feet across and twice that distance upward totally encompassing the meeting hall and everything in it became as hot as is the interior of the sun, and was subjected to a pressure force of thirty million pounds per square inch.

The pressure tore outward, converting what it touched to superheated gas. The tiny heart of that momentary star erupted into savaging atomic energy, at the same instant the powder in the bullet of the gun held by Jomo Mwanza exploded.

The bullet never fired. In that instant it ceased to exist.

Exposed to the heart of a star, the bullet, the gun, every man, the entire building, the ground on which it stood, the earth and air about it became energy. Molecular structure vanished in the flicker of time that the atom raged—the visible fireball still to follow. It was a moment, had one been able to measure the passage of events, that could have had as its yardstick the bullet in Jomo Mwanza's gun: before it reached the muzzle of the gun it no longer existed.

Butukama was suddenly in a naked glare that spread instantly through the city, and began the slow process of chemical combustion on nearly every surface it touched. Behind that savage light came the exploding fireball and the shock wave that moved sideward and downward, slammed into the earth, gouging a hemispherical depression, sledgehammering beyond, rolling the crust of the earth within its reach as if it were so much jelly.

Above ground the blazing fireball expanded in a fraction of a second to form a dome of energy, glowing too brightly at first to be seen and then, as it cooled within seconds, showing a mottled form of berserk power expanding, pulsating, contracting. From the edge of the fireball erupted the shock wave, still with a pressure of many tons to the square inch.

Butukama vanished.

They saw it from the jet thirteen miles high and more than a hundred miles to the north.

The pilot flying the DH-125 had put on thick, almost opaque smoked glasses. Through this glass the naked sun, even stared at directly, was only the faintest, barely discernible glow. Yet what took place shook the pilot so that he would never forget it.

A commercial jetliner en route to South Africa flew over two hours after the blast. Most of the cloud was by then dissipated, a harmless-looking spray of white in the very high air. The crew and passengers saw fires burning, drifting smoke.

A gaping crater looked up at them.

CHAPTER 5

Three seconds after the atomic bomb annihilated what had been the city of Butukama, sensors contained within two Vela Hotel satellites orbiting seventy-four thousand miles above the earth registered the stellar light flash of the exploding atomic bomb. Because the heavy cloud cover and rain as well as the bomb being exploded slightly beneath the surface held down the sudden burst of light, the Vela Hotel satellites delayed flashing the alert signal to ground receiving stations. The computerized systems judged what they detected in the visible spectrum and then compared other radiation signatures of the nuclear energy release.

The first detection of the blast by the Vela Hotels did not require three seconds. Such detection was instantaneous. But the satellites had been prepared with redundant systems so that any immediate activation of the sensors as a result of faulty equipment would not trigger combat alarms in the main space data control center in the Rocky Mountains.

The first satellite ran through a review of its detection of the visible and other radiation signature and then flashed word of what had been received. With that alert signal went a complete review of the time continuity of the events, and, also, a complete report on the equipment used by the satellite in detecting, registering, checking and then signalling what had happened. The message flashed from the Vela Hotel not to the earth antenna which, at that moment, was not in direct range between satellite and

40

earth station, but to seven military communications satellites in geosynchronous orbit at average distances from the earth of some 23,000 miles. The use of seven satellites was also a matter of redundancy, since signal transmission and retransmission was automatic.

At the same moment the alert message was moving through the computer processing system of the North American Air Defense Command (NORAD) deep in the bowels of a Colorado mountain, the second Vela Hotel completed processing its own detection, checkout and transmission signal, and was relaying its report through the military comsats to Colorado.

These first two messages that there had just occurred the uncontrolled release of nuclear energy above the earth, and that this energy was from a complete fission process rather than an exploding nuclear pile or some other such nonmilitary system, required another thirty-one seconds to be flashed on the readout panel of the combat center of the North American Air Defense Command. The readout came in several forms. One took place on a large wall screen where the printout message was "frozen." TV transmission of that screen took place automatically to all appropriate control center desks within NORAD. At the same time, other readouts were taking place through telex, printed circuit and related systems.

Through automatic alerting communications nets, the news from the Vela Hotels was also flashed simultaneously to the White House, the combined services combat intelligence center in the Pentagon and headquarters of the Strategic Air Command in Nebraska. Dissemination of the message was made with the warning:

THIS NUCLEAR DETONATION ALERT REQUIRES FURTHER CONFIRMATION. DO NOT REPEAT DO NOT ACTIVATE ANY COMBAT EMERGENCY PROCEDURES BEYOND PREPLANNED NOTIFICATION UNTIL CONFIRMING MESSAGE IS TRANSMITTED THROUGH NORAD. DO NOT REQUEST INFORMATION AT THIS POINT. STAND BY FOR MESSAGE CONFIRMATION.

It required another two minutes, nineteen seconds for

the NORAD combat control center duty officer to interrogate the Vela Hotel satellites for computer reconfirmation of the original messages. A repeat signal, taped within the satellites, also flashed on command, and the two messages were compared within the NORAD computers. Moments later reconfirmation flashed from the computers, and a sergeant began tapping out the second message dictated to him by the colonel on duty.

> GREENAPPLE TWO CONFIRMATION NUCLEAR DETONA-
> TION ALERT. DETECTION BY TWO REPEAT TWO VELA
> HOTEL SATELLITES ALPHA NINER AND DELTA SIX,
> COMPLETE COMPUTER VERIFICATION SIGNALS. FUR-
> THER DATA FOLLOWS. CLOSEST POPULATION CENTER
> IMMEDIATE GROSS ESTIMATES VELA HOTEL COORDI-
> NATES IS BUTUKAMA IN CONGO, CONTINENT AFRICA.
> MESSAGE LIST BRAVO FOXTROT IS NOW ACTIVATED,
> INTERROGATION DETAILS THIS CENTER CONTACT CODE
> FLYBY PROTON SEVEN SEVEN TANGO. MESSAGE ENDS.

Another office in NORAD headquarters immediately began its own message transmissions along a standing notification list. The exact contents of both messages from NORAD was now disseminated through hotline and other systems to the Tactical Air Command, Army Combat Headquarters, Navy Combat Headquarters, the Federal Aviation Administration, the Office of Civil Defense, and sixty-seven other separate notification points. This list was a primary notification requirement aside from what any government agency or division might do on its own.

"That's everything so far."

Colonel Milton Hawkins studied the papers in front of him. At his right side was a nuclear weapons expert from the Department of Defense. To his left, a weapons scientist from the Atomic Energy Commission and an expert on Russian affairs sat around the long conference table in the basement of the White House. Colonel Hawkins was the military aide to the President. He had already alerted the chief executive but would not contact him again until he had every available bit of information. More than information he needed expert opinion to evaluate the facts to date.

"Dr. Jameson, what do you make of this so far?" Colonel Hawkins asked. The AEC scientist hesitated, then: "It appears to be a single detonation of an intermediate to high-yield fission weapon. It also seems to be a high-technology product. Initial indications point to a surface or a low sub-surface burst, which means high downwind fallout. I'd say the yield was on the order of two to five hundred kilotons."

"You say a high-technology product, Doctor. Why?"

"When you get that kind of yield from a fission bomb you've got something that was put together by a weapons laboratory."

Colonel Hawkins glanced at his air force counterpart. "Bob, you agree?"

"Down the line. When we get a look through some other systems we can sift more facts from extrapolation. We're trying to get air samples of the cloud. When we do, even the preliminary reports will tell us much more . . . damn near right down to the serial number."

"Is it possible it's one of our own missing bombs?"

"Possible. Can't tell yet. We've got to break down the fission products we'll pick up in cloud sampling."

Hawkins turned to his communications officer. "Do we have confirmation of message receipt from Moscow?"

"Yes, sir. It's gone to the President."

Colonel Hawkins thought of the old days and what might have happened when an atomic bomb went off in the world, away from a testing ground, and he felt a chill pass through him.

He rose to his feet. "Gentlemen, thank you for your patience. I'd appreciate it if you would stand by just a bit longer."

He walked quickly down the hall to see the President.

That night the CIA activated its world-wide reporting system throughout the world, following every lead that might possibly tie the blast in Butukama with any move made by the Soviet Union, directly or indirectly. This was not carried out under the suspicion that the Soviets might be responsible for the mysterious explosion, but was, rather, following through with standard procedure. If the thorough, world-wide checkout failed to indicate a link to the Russians, so much the better.

The White House, following long-established procedures, notified the Kremlin of detection of a nuclear blast through two hot lines, one of cable and the other through the military comsat net orbiting the planet. The equivalent agencies of the Soviet Union, again following a procedure agreed upon by both governments, had done the same. The Russian response to the explosion was delayed only slightly as compared to the extensive American detection system, but the messages passing between Washington and Moscow indicated the preparation behind the set-up.

Every nuclear submarine of both nations had been alerted that an event of unusual and potentially dangerous significance had taken place. Every nuclear submarine went to Yellow Alert at once; it was a response both effective and well-contained. Political events had brought on many more Condition Yellow alerts than had military moves.

Parallel reactions took place in the complexes of silo-contained ICBMs of both nations. A total of 2,784 missiles carrying hydrogen bombs also went to Condition Yellow, which stopped short of arming the warheads.

The only immediate *active* response occurred with manned aircraft. In the United States a total of thirty-nine B-52 bombers swung from their orbiting stations over the United States and Canada to demarcation lines closer to the borders of the Soviet Union. Ordnance officers aboard the heavy jet bombers brought the two massive hydrogen bombs of each airplane from stand-down status to initial interlock.

Every man knew that approximately the same steps were being followed by their counterparts in large airplanes bearing the markings of the USSR.

Jackson McKay hurried his bulk through the final corridor to his office. He had enough time in the tire-squealing rush to his office to review everything received so far on the atomic blast, and he was impatient for information from the follow-up systems.

He realized suddenly that Oscar Goldman was not there.

"Where the hell is Goldman?" he asked his secretary.

"Colorado, Mr. McKay. You remember, sir, he went with Colonel Austin."

Of course. Well, he thought, yesterday the concept of using atomic bombs for limited political objectives had been only theory. Today it seemed likely to have become much more than that. With the proliferation of capacity among countries and the responsible presumption of stolen nuclear materials and weapons, the threat of superpower confrontation was much less—just as the opportunity for small and independent groups or countries was much greater. Austin, he decided, was going to be launched on his mission sooner than expected.

He turned to his secretary. "Set up contact with BCE as soon as you can. Before they reply, be sure they have everything up to date with their counterparts so they can brief me on the latest. Also, get hold of Stetz at Nuke and ask him to do the same." Imagine, he thought, the Americans and Russians in harness to track down an outlaw atom blast. . . .

Three hundred miles off the west coast of Africa, far from sight of land, Sam Franks slid behind the control yoke in the left seat of the DH-125. For a long moment he sat quietly, his eyes taking in every detail of the instruments before him. He held his gaze on a blinking red light. Directly above the light a needle pointed to the left, crossing a wider double-lined marker. A digital counter read out the numbers eighty-two. Eighty-two miles separation from the Boeing and they were intersecting with forty-degree closure.

Franks glanced to the copilot on his right. "What's their altitude?" he asked.

"Thirty-nine."

"Can they hold?"

"They're holding."

Franks digested it. Thirty-nine thousand feet was a little high for what they planned but the man flying the Boeing was good. Sam Franks had checked him out personally.

Franks moved his right hand to the autopilot, adjusted a control. Almost imperceptibly at this height, the nose of the DH-125 eased below the horizon. Two thousand feet a minute. The mach needle slid a notch higher to the red line marked on its dial. Franks glanced again at the digital readout above the blinking red light. The eighty-two had changed to a sixty-three. They were closing fast, and he increased slightly their rate of descent.

They picked up the contrail barely a minute later, a broad swath through the lower stratosphere. The long white ribbon slashed across the sky to their left, still well below their own altitude. Franks waited. Finally he leaned forward with his left hand on the yoke. "Kill the auto," he told the copilot. He waited until the autopilot system had been disconnected from the controls before he released a tight grip on the yoke. Experience had taught him you never knew when something in that computer might foul up and the ship go berserk because of a fouled trim when you shifted back to manual. He also wanted the feel of the ship in his hands before closing to the Boeing.

The 707 slid into view, a wide-winged silver minnow racing ahead of its contrail. Franks adjusted the thin pencil mike before his lips and pressed the transmit button on the yoke. "Grey Eagle, we have visual. Six miles."

"Roger, Pineapple. Confirm visual and six. You're closing nicely."

Franks kept narrowing the distance until he could read the bright red lettering across the fuselage of the big Boeing. Turkish Cargolines. That name would disappear minutes after the Boeing rolled into a hangar at its distant destination.

"Grey Eagle, let's get on with it."

"Wilco, Pineapple. Remain alongside."

"Roger."

Franks glanced to his left. A blister extended slowly beneath the aft belly of the 707. It reached its full length of travel and a funnel slid away slowly at the end of a telescoping boom, kept from rotational or other movement by two slab fins. He waited for the call from the big airplane.

"Pineapple, probe extended and we're ready."

Franks waited several moments, studying the refueling boom behind the Boeing. It was all in the slot. "Okay, Grey Eagle. We're dropping behind and coming in." He moved a toggle switch in the center of the panel. The DH-125 swayed slightly and vibrated as an access door above and behind Franks opened in the powerful wind. Moments later the vibration increased as a refueling boom extended into view above and to his left.

He skillfully closed the remaining distance. The boom slid into the waiting probe and a green light snapped on. "How's your light?" Franks asked.

This time the fueling engineer responded. "We're green and go, Pineapple. You ready?"

"Roger, let's have it."

Seven minutes later the fuel tanks of the DH-125 read full. Franks called in the information and the fueling engineer confirmed fuel flow off and ready for disconnect. Franks eased off power. The DH-125 disconnected and Franks broke away to the right, brought power in and slid alongside the Boeing until the refueling boom was fully retracted and the blister brought back into the Boeing.

"Grey Eagle, you're clean," Franks said.

He knew the Boeing crew was studying his own ship. "Roger that, Pineapple. You show the same."

"Have a good trip," Franks said. He rolled in nose up trim, added power, and the DH-125 went for upstairs again. They'd land in an isolated field seventy miles north of the port city of Cagliari in Sardinia while the 707 flew on to an equally isolated field in Turkey.

It had been an interesting morning, thought Franks. He turned the ship back to the copilot and the ever-waiting robot brain and went back into the cabin, where five minutes later he was sound asleep.

CHAPTER 6

Now they were all brought into operation.

The first were the Vela Hotel watchdogs in their ceaseless surveillance for a nuclear explosion anywhere above the earth's surface.

A Camelot satellite, one of four in polar orbit, signalled detection of sudden radiation in the infrared band. The report went into the NORAD computers with the original Vela Hotel flash, confirming the nature of the detonation as well as providing additional confirmation of geographical coordinates.

A Ferret satellite, scanning frequency bands necessary for certain types of military systems, was interrogated as it passed within line-of-sight range of a ground receiving station. The time of detonation reported by the Vela Hotel and Camelot satellites was computer-checked with the time-related signals recorded by the Ferret. Within seconds the computer technician stared at a "bogey" signal recorded on tape. He punched into the computer the new information and passed on the word to Combat Center inside NORAD. The signal was further computer-checked across a wide range of special electronic transmissions until there seemed little doubt.

Which called for additional electronic sleuthing.

Six Samos and one Big Eye military reconnaissance satellites were in orbit at the time of the atomic blast. Interrogation began immediately. One Samos satellite within line-of-sight of the Butukama area, covering an area slightly to the north and well to the south of the geograph-

48

ical coordinates of the city, was commanded to initiate its on-board film processor. Film taken by the Eastman-Kodak search-and-find camera system was developed and printed and, as the Samos passed over a ground station, the pictures flashed to the NORAD center in Colorado, confirming a dark-textured mushroom cloud ascending through the heavy cloud cover in the Butukama area.

That confirmation initiated immediate tracking of the radioactive cloud dissipating rapidly downwind of Butukama. Within two hours three SR-71 reconnaissance planes descended from 80,000 feet and punched through the cloud. The planes returned to 30,000 feet where they refueled from KC-135 tankers, and raced toward the United States with filter traps containing particles from the radioactive cloud drifting away from Butukama. Five nuclear submarines were ordered to move at once to positions along a line that would permit further surface sampling of fallout particles. Careful study of the particles would provide a detailed composition of the type of bomb material and even the design of the weapon, although the latter would require much more time.

Three days prior to the Butukama disaster the United States Air Force had launched from the Western Test Range in California a huge Titan-3D/Agena booster with a ten-ton, fifty-foot-long Big Bird reconnaissance satellite, equipped with both an Eastman-Kodak search-and-find camera system and a giant Perkin-Elmer close-look camera. Within one hour and forty-three minutes of the atomic explosion, the Big Bird orbited along a line from north to south nearly a thousand miles west of Butukama. All camera systems were activated and as fast as pictures were developed, they were processed aboard the satellite and radio-transmitted to the military receiving system. If the initial pictures proved useful, on a succeeding orbital pass permanent photographs would be taken, after which the satellite would be ground-commanded to eject a small re-entry capsule with the original negatives aboard.

The initial radioed pictures revealed a find that at first seemed to have no bearing on the nuclear explosion. Two contrails appeared some three hundred miles west of the African coast, but they were simply part of a contrail pattern involving many jet aircraft operating at high altitude. The pictures would have remained worthless except for the skill of an intelligence officer who believed in checking out *any* possibility, no matter how remote.

Two hours later the intelligence officer studied the computer report. He requested a complete rundown on all information received so far on the explosion. When he finished scanning the assembled data he referred again to the photograph from the Big Bird satellite. Five minutes later he was in the office of the NORAD intelligence chief to explain his findings.

It was simple enough and it *might* not have meant anything. But it did.

First, the contrails appearing on the photographs had been fed into the computer. These were then cross-checked with every airline flight and route to eliminate the majority of contrails; such aircraft were fully accounted for. Telephone and telex messages to the appropriate authorities in several countries produced the flight plan records of other aircraft, not included in airline schedules. This accounted for cargo flights and a number of business and private aircraft, all of which were required to file flight plans and maintain progress according to those plans. Deviations were noted and recorded.

Two aircraft failed to fit within the scope of the careful review. With all other aircraft and their contrails eliminated it was possible to select the two white lines on the photographs for which no flight plans or other identification was known. The photographs were rushed to the computer center for enhancement of detail. Placed within special enlargers they gave up their secret.

"We have positive identification," the intelligence officer explained, "of the larger aircraft. A Boeing 707. No question about that. There's sufficient clarity in the picture to show the sweepback at thirty-five degrees instead of thirty as with a DC-8. That, and some other details. See here? The distance between the wing leading edge to the nose, and from the trailing edge to where the tail begins. The intercontinental version, the 320 series, is considerably larger in fuselage length, so we should be right on target with both the aircraft type and basic model. I think we

50

can even break it down to one of the original 707-120 models." The men surrounding him showed their disbelief. "The contrail. There's a distinct pattern to the type of engine. It's not the type of trail you get from the turbofan engine. It's the older turbojet. That's reinforced by the fact that the trail even shows another signature. The original J-57 engines on the early 707 airplanes, at least a lot of them, were fitted with a particular type of noise suppressor. Some are still in service. I've checked the trail patterns for these aircraft and they are different, sufficiently so, to get a good handle on them." His finger tapped the pictures. "It fits," said the officer, "it fits all the way."

He was asked, "What about the other ship?"

"Smaller. Twin-engine. I checked out the location at the time of every possible small four-engine ship like the Lockheed Jetstar. All accounted for. That makes this one pretty well defined as a business-type jet with two aft engines and a high horizontal stabilizer. See the shadow across the stabilizer of the 707? It's not there with the other airplane, yet they were both photographed with the same angle to the sun. So we're looking at a high horizontal tail."

Silence. Then an officer turned to him, shaking his head. "You wouldn't happen to know the pilot's name, would you?"

Next came old-fashioned detective work. Into the computer went the maximum range possible of the two airplanes as determined by their position from the nearest airport. All possible landing sites within that range went into a new programming for the computer. Alternate possibilities of air refueling the smaller jet were then fed into the computer. A team of more than a hundred intelligence specialists began to track down the landing and ground movement of every Boeing 707-120, and a jet of the general characteristics of the machine in the photographs with the Boeing. It was drudgery and it was painstaking and it never paid off.

Nothing. The two airplanes had simply vanished.

Which was its own kind of message.

Airplanes did not simply disappear.

Not, that is, unless there was an organization with the means to make it happen.

Jackson McKay hoped he had an answer. Its name was Cyborg Steve Austin. The time for his launching was now.

CHAPTER 7

A television studio . . . Steve Austin moving stiffly, slowly, across the stage to the waiting host. The public hadn't seen Steve since that terrible desert crash at least a year ago. They remembered him as "the last man to walk the moon," young, tall, rugged-handsome. The studio audience and home viewers were startled by the scarred face, the strained look of this man who had lost his legs and an arm and God knew what else . . . well, at least there wouldn't be any more talk that he had died, and as for being crippled forever, well, they said the doctors could do miracles and there was one right in front of them.

"Life Is Wonderful!" was the country's new TV talk show and it was even putting worry lines on NBC executives as it nearly pulled even with Johnny Carson. Emcee Bob Harvey had apparently pulled off a coup in getting as his special guest the last man on the moon, a man who had seemed to disappear from the earth, a man they'd said would be a basket case the rest of his life, if indeed he'd survived at all. Bob Harvey's opposition called him superschlock but Harvey had apparently grabbed the brass ring, carried along on the wave of nostalgia that was washing over America. This was *the* night. Steve Austin could put him right over the top. Even Carson would want to watch *this*. And—for added excitement—this particular show would be *live,* not taped, by specific request of Austin's representatives (he wasn't sure just who they were but who cared). His producer was a bit put off by that, but you didn't argue with the kind of booking that could make the show number one.

Harvey's other guest was a man as big physically as he was at the box office, and also making a rare TV appearance. Movie hero for two decades, Duane Barker was also an outspoken conservative; his critics called it right-wing reactionary. He was a winner and presumably just the sort of real man to help greet Austin. One patriot to another ... When the tumult of applause finally calmed, Bob Harvey faced the main camera and said, "We have another guest. His name is Marty Sehiller. When you see him, you'll feel the way I did when I learned that this man has no legs. But more important, he's also the man who taught his friend, Steve Austin, how to walk with artificial limbs. I give you ... Marty Schiller!"

Jackson McKay slouched in his leather chair. To his right Oscar Goldman leaned forward. They watched the television screen without a word between them as Marty Schiller moved across the stage, the cameras following every move. Where Steve Austin had seemed to have some difficulty and pain, Schiller was a giant of a man who gave off a sense of great strength. Massive shoulders and thick arms, a toothy grin, huge and calloused hands—and when they thought of *this* man having no legs of his own, well, it was almost too much. . . . Schiller stood quietly by Steve Austin while the crowd screamed. Again. When all was finally quiet Bob Harvey, voice tight, told the audience about Schiller. Ex-paratrooper, underwater demolition expert . . . and when he told how Marty Schiller, legs blown away by a land mine, came back not only to walk but to teach other men to do the same, including this famous ex-astronaut . . .

Oscar Goldman glanced at Jackson McKay. "What do you think?"

"I think," he said, "I am going to be sick."

Goldman smiled. "Don't knock it. After all, we wrote the script."

The show started as a guaranteed winner. After the introductions it was downhill all the way. The awesome canyon Duane Barker used for a mouth that night was unprecedented—even for him. Hollywood's hero brought up Steve Austin straight in his chair when he declared his pleasure at the moon program being ended. "Waste of money," Barker said, and at the same time proclaimed his deep pride at what America had accomplished in Vietnam —and would accomplish in the future against aggression. He bowed to Marty Schiller. "Pride is what I have for men like you," boomed the box-office sensation.

Schiller stared at him in seeming disbelief.

"You have got to be," Steve Austin said, slowly and distinctly, "the most stupid and pompous ass I have ever met."

Live television. All across America. Austin was the man who'd come back from the moon, from the *dead*. He was entitled to have his say . . . The studio engineers looked at one another, nodded and grinned. They'd been told this might be a hot one, but to let it run unless they got a special signal. Austin and Schiller were untouchable, heroes . . .

Duane Barker drew himself up to his full six feet six inches and stared down at Steve Austin. "In view of your previous service, Colonel, and the fact that you *are* handicapped, I'll try to overlook that, because otherwise I swear to you I'd—"

Oscar Goldman stared intently at the TV screen. "Now, Steve. Use the left arm . . ."

Steve was on his feet, facing Duane Barker. For a moment he turned to his side, looking at Marty Schiller. The big man rose slowly and his hands came up from his sides, palms up. He shrugged.

Steve turned back to Barker, started forward and stumbled, and in the same motion brought up his right hand to grab Barker's tie. This brought the big man stooping forward, off balance. And made his face a target for a bionics arm.

They would need to play it back slow motion to see the

54

arm move and Steve's left fist connect with Barker's nose, snapping his head back wildly. By the time Steve released his grip on the man's tie, Barker was unconscious, and collapsing full out on the stage floor.

Bob Harvey yelled for them to stop it and started toward Steve. As he did so, an oversized hand snapped out, grabbed him by the back of his legs, and with dramatic ease picked Harvey from the floor, held him kicking frantically, then dumped him from sight behind the couch.

By now members of the network security force were on the scene. Schiller met the first with an open-handed *smack* across the face that somersaulted the man. Steve took another with a sudden body bend, catching the man with one hand by his jacket and with his other hand grasping him between the legs. Steve, using the other's momentum, tossed him over his head. He collapsed in a heap some ten feet beyond. The remaining guards, not unreasonably, hesitated, and Marty Schiller grabbed Steve, pointed to the rear exit from the stage. They took it and rushed down the emergency stairway to the ground floor.

As they went through the door to the street a wall of reporters and TV lights was already in place. A police car pulled up and two officers bulled their way through. Flashguns popped in dazzling succession as Steve took one and Schiller the other. They pushed past the policemen, and Schiller let loose with an ear-piercing whistle at a cab across the street. Newsmen at their heels, they shoved into the cab. "Just get the hell out of here," Steve said. The cab shot away from the curb with the door still not completely closed.

They were six blocks away before anyone spoke. "Wow," the driver said, "ain't you two sumpin'!" He glanced at them in his mirror. "I seen the whole thing. They had a special big TV set in front of the studio. Saw it all. Man, you two . . ." They saw the grin on his face.

Schiller leaned forward. "How's your sense of direction?" he asked.

"Lousy. What you got in mind?"

"Kennedy airport. The maintenance hangars. We've . . . got some friends there."

"Done," said the cabbie. "You mind some advice?"

"Shoot."

"We don't go to the airport. Not direct, I mean. Too obvious. We can't take the tunnels. You know, the toll booths. Maybe they already got my number. So we take the 59th Street bridge. From there I can hit the Northern State Parkway and go past the airport, cut south to the Southern State Parkway. We feed right into the Belt, and we make it to the field from the other direction."

Steve glanced at Marty Schiller, who nodded. "Go," Schiller said. "And thanks. Anyway, it'll be a good fare."

The driver turned to him. "You think you had a fight on your hands tonight? You two jokers try to pay *me,* and you'll know what a fight really is."

The cabbie worked the back roads of the sprawling airport and let them off near a side door to the giant maintenance hangar of Pan American Airways. They made it to the locker room. At one end of the room was a large laundry bin. Moments later each of them was wearing a soiled maintenance overall. They went back outside, away from the interior of the brightly lit hangar, walking casually to the flight ramp.

Steve nudged Marty Schiller, nodded toward a work crew that was preparing to tow a Boeing 707 from the maintenance line to the passenger terminal. "You can get a lot of time for hijacking."

"Who the hell is hijacking?" Schiller said. "We're *stealing.*"

Steve laughed. "Never thought of it that way. Let's go."

They clambered up the workstand and entered the jetliner. A mechanic looked at them from the cockpit, and Marty Schiller waved urgently for the man to come back into the cabin. Moments later he was lowered gently, unconscious, into a passenger seat. Steve went to the flight deck. Minutes later he gestured to Schiller. "It's all here. Fueled and serviced for the run to Paris, capacity for a full passenger load."

"Charts?" Schiller asked, and nodded with satisfaction when Steve pointed to a bulging case.

"All here," Steve told him.

They carried the unconscious mechanic to the work

stand, shouted to a ground crewman that the mechanic was sick and to roll back the stand. Schiller also told the man they had orders to run up the engines and taxi for several minutes and he wanted everything clear. By the time he returned to the cockpit Steve was strapped into the left seat, headset about his ears, going through the check list. The big jets started easily. For another minute Steve held position, studying the gauges, then gestured for Schiller to put on his own headset.

"We'll taxi as long as we can with the main door open," Steve told him. "When I say go, you close it, fast."

Steve listened to ground control, got the active runway situated in his mind and started rolling. They were still a thousand yards away from it when someone at PAA got the word to the tower. "We got company," Schiller said, pointing to his right. Emergency lights. Vehicles racing to them. Steve gave Schiller the word to close the door. He went to tower frequency.

"Kennedy Tower, PAA Niner-Six here. We have an emergency. Repeat, we have an emergency. We are taking the next intersection onto the active. Clear the runway of all landing and take-off traffic. I repeat, clear the runway of all landing and take-off traffic." He didn't wait for an answer, rolling sharply to the right onto the main runway. A huge shape thundered over them as the tower shouted for a landing airliner to make an emergency go-around. Steve hit the brakes, turning left, drifting to the right side of the runway. They'd need the full three thousand feet of extra distance with this ship. At the runway's end he swung the big Boeing into a tight left turn, straightened out the nosewheel, scanned the gauges.

By his side he heard Schiller say, "Anybody for Europe?"

"Why not," Steve said, and edged the throttles forward, standing on the brakes. Flashing lights came toward them. "Hang on," Steve said, releasing the brakes and snapping on blazing landing lights. The Boeing lurched forward, accelerating swiftly. The chasing vehicles shot to the sides of the runway to escape the monster bearing down on them.

They watched helplessly as the huge jet rose into the sky.

57

Their whole emergency system was set up to deal with hijacking. The alert team met in the airport director's office, tied in with hot lines to Air Traffic Control and to McGuire Air Force Base in New Jersey. The Pan American director of flight operations was in a maddening conversation with the Air Force fighter controller at McGuire.

"But, sir, if it's not a hijacking—"

"That's right," the PAA man said, "they *stole* the airplane! Do you understand?"

"Yes, sir. That means no passengers. We already have two fighters scrambled. They're closing in now. We're prepared to order the men to turn back or—"

"Or *what?* Major, that airplane cost ten million dollars! *Ten million!* Are you going to pay for the damned thing?"

"Steve. Off to my right." Marty Schiller pointed. "You can just make them out. Two of them, it looks like. Fighters."

Steve banked the 707 for a better view. "One-oh-sixes, in fact."

"Any ideas?"

"They'll come alongside. Fly a tight formation. Then they'll call us on the emergency frequency and warn us to turn back."

"Then what?"

"They got nice people flying those planes, Marty. Wave to them."

Which is what Schiller did as the F-106 pilots got their orders from McGuire, peeled off and went home.

The alert team at Kennedy airport heard the telephone ring. The PAA man jerked the phone from its cradle and snapped his name.

"Bad news," a voice said. "There's a big front over the Atlantic. They're in it by now. We've lost all contact."

The PAA man lowered the phone slowly.

"They're gone," he said.

CHAPTER 8

The members of the hastily convened United Nations Study of the Side Effects of the Unspecified Nuclear Disaster in Africa had just departed, much to McKay's relief. Maybe now they could get down to it.

"Anybody have anything more on the device itself?" He glanced about the table. Charles D. Strong from BCE. The letters came from the letter-numbers of uranium 235, the three numbers corresponding to the second, third and fifth letters of the alphabet. BCE worked as an arm of the American government with the unusual responsibility of coordinating with its opposite number, Atomik, in Moscow, to keep track of international marketing of nuclear devices. It served more as a clearing house than it did as an intelligence organization, but simply gathering and sifting through information had become such a stupendous job that other agencies welcomed the filtering service of BCE. Charlie Strong served another useful purpose; heading an organization that functioned with the blessings of Moscow, he could maintain a working liaison with Interpol without incurring the distrust of the Russians, who also worked with the international police group.

Alongside Strong of BCE was Drew Stetz from the NUKE office. Stetz played the same role in secret intelligence that Strong did openly with the Russians and the international community. The NUKE people had accounted for—to date—more than seventy nuclear devices lost, stolen or misplaced through remarkably intricate record-keeping.

59

Arthur Castalini represented Interpol. He was a no-nonsense professional policeman, and he and McKay had worked together back in the Second World War. Castalini was there wearing the hat of Lisbon director of Interpol—a neat trick for an Italian.

Two more men made up the conference group. Val Phillips of CIA and Tim Henderson of the Defense Department. Henderson represented all the services and their combined intelligence departments. McKay respected him.

"All right," said Val Phillips, "let's have it, Jackson. *What* is going on with Steve Austin? We've just had an atom bomb exploded by some outfit in Africa and right in the middle of the flap about that one of your favorite projects happens to go haywire and get international headline publicity—"

"He was not one of our people," McKay broke in. "I've no time to quibble over details of experimental programs with you, Val—" McKay paused, wondering how much of this would be repeated one way or another by Castalini when he returned to Europe. "But what we were planning with Austin was no secret among the agencies . . . You know what we do with amputees. If their other attributes fit our needs we train them for special jobs. Steve Austin, because of his unique background, held great possibilities for us. But it didn't work out," McKay said with sarcasm, "as you can perhaps tell from the headlines."

Phillips smiled. "The project did not work out, and yet this man is capable of decking somebody nearly twice his size, stealing a 707, and flying it out of the country? Look, we can take this up later if you want, Jackson, but we know you spent over a million on Austin and—"

"*Six* million," McKay corrected him, "and before you further reveal your lack of information, I recommend you brief yourself on a man called Douglas Bader."

Phillips showed the question on his face, and Castalini joined in. "Maybe I can help out, Mr. Phillips. The name Douglas Bader is very well known to us in Europe. During World War II he was one of England's greatest aces. A brilliant fighter pilot."

Phillips didn't like the crossfire. "Your point?"

"Douglas Bader had no legs. His artificial limbs were of

60

metal and wood. He shot down all the enemy planes *after* the accident that severed both his legs. By the way, there were eight other pilots in that war who flew with artificial legs. But Mr. Bader is more relevant to the Austin story. Bader was also notorious for trying to break out of German prison camps." Castalini nodded to McKay. "My apologies. It was really none of my business."

McKay waved aside the apology. Val Phillips was off balance and McKay enjoyed that. "You might also call Marty Schiller a failure," he said to the CIA man. "If you recall, he and Austin took off together."

Phillips made a last try. "You said you spent six million dollars on Austin. What for?"

"We built a testing laboratory," McKay said wearily. "It was for an entire program. It was coordinated with the Air Force, the Veterans Administration, three hospitals specializing in amputee and paraplegic rehabilitation and—" McKay shook his head. "Look, Val. Austin and Schiller are now being hunted as dangerous criminals. They are no longer my worry. *Or* yours. Now, do you mind if we get on with it?"

"We have been searching down a very good lead," Castalini told them. "By using a combination of all the facilities at our disposal, which includes everything from computers to an old, wrinkled woman from Naples who uses garlic to tell the future"—he shrugged—"who knows, we must leave *nothing* to chance, any of us. Well, we pursued this lead and it had much to do with aircraft. Especially international cargo flights. There seemed to be pilots from different countries involved. It could have been ordinary, but it did merit attention."

Tim Henderson of the Defense Department pushed for more. "Any luck, Arthur?"

"We did discover a very large flying organization. It has bases throughout southern Europe. We also are of the opinion that there is no purpose to be served in further investigation."

"Why not?" Henderson persisted.

"For one thing, it seems completely legitimate, however extensive and profitable its freight and other operations. And if our suspicions ever should be confirmed," Castalini said with a grimace, "then the atomic weapon that destroyed Butukama was exploded by the Italian government." He smiled without humor. "The base, the facility we finally tracked down? It was a field of the Italian Air Force. And we Italians are very frightened of atomic bombs, may I add." Castalini glanced from Henderson to McKay. "I don't mean to sound frivolous, but I did need to impress on you that our biggest lead to date doesn't seem worth much."

"I understand, and thank you," McKay said. "Still, we need *something,* gentlemen, if only to take the pressure off the President about our own CIA."

"Don't misunderstand," McKay said quickly. "The Soviet premier has talked directly with the President. The premier said that his intelligence services had concluded that an international group dealing in nuclear devices definitely exists." McKay shifted position in his chair. "If you'll recall, Val, there have been occasions in the past when the CIA did establish various front organizations to serve its purposes. In any case, the premier did everything but come right out and say the international group handling such weapons is really a blind created by the CIA. The accusation is that the United States is now playing international criminal politics."

To McKay's surprise there was no angry reaction from the CIA man. Phillips said quietly, "That's very funny. That was the conclusion *we* came to about the Russians."

CHAPTER 9

The two men slipped quietly along the chipped concrete wall of the warehouse, stealthy yet sure of themselves. They paused at the corner of the building, flattened
against the wall, taking stock of their position. The second
man questioned his companion with a glance; the other
nodded slightly. Voices carried through fog from a distance, and the Naples waterfront vibrated with the rasping
horns of ships moving with heightened caution in the gray
mists. It was time. The lead figure motioned and like two
wraiths the men reached a thick, large metal door. The
second man brought into view a microtorch. They shielded
the intense pinpoint of flame with their coats as they
burned not through the door but through a concrete section to reach the alarm tripwires. Seconds later the wires
were disconnected and the door alarm rendered useless.
They eased into the warehouse, closed the door silently
behind them. Each man took out a revolver from a
shoulder holster. They started slowly forward.

"They aren't bad," Sam Franks said, looking at the television screen that monitored the two men by a closed-
circuit scanning system as they now moved into the warehouse. Franks lit his cigar and turned to Jonathan Sperry.
Meticulous in his appearance, Sperry watched as the two
intruders worked their way into another room.

"Interesting," Sperry said. "It's not often I see anything
more than the paperwork. Do we receive many visitors of
this sort?"

"Not so often in the past. Lately it's almost on schedule. They're trying to close the ring on us."

"Do you ever find out who sent them?"

Franks, showing slight irritation at any questioning of his security procedures, said, "At least half."

"I didn't intend to offend, Sam, but how do you manage that? They wouldn't carry any identification."

"Fingerprints, mug shots, identifying scars. We make up multiple copies and check them out with Interpol, NATO, other security groups. Our contact in NATO, for example, can fan out requests to any NATO member country, where there's always somebody ready to make an extra buck—" He cut himself short as the men on the TV monitor worked their way into a third room.

"The screen will go blank for a few moments," Franks went on, referring to the drama unfolding in front of them. "Flash bombs. Four in the room, in each corner. That way no matter where they happen to be looking we get them. If one of them has his eyes closed, blink reflex opens them. The flashes are ripple-pattern so they get a full dose. They're blind afterward."

"Permanent?"

"Don't know. They don't stay alive long enough to find out. There's the warning signal. Don't bother about the screen. There's an automatic overload cutoff for high light intensity, then the picture comes back on. There—"

They watched the two men crossing a room. Behind them a door left partially open slammed shut. Instantly the men swung around, guns ready. The next moment the TV monitor screen went blank. When the picture came on again several seconds later the men were staggering about in obvious agony.

Even Jonathan Sperry, experienced in other men's deaths, felt his lips go dry. A door on the far side of the room was hurled away from its latch, and through the open space charged a pack of huge, ravening Dobermans. The guns were useless. Meticulously trained, the dogs operated in two teams, three to a team. Each dog had a particular vital spot to attack. One, the genitals; another, the wrist holding a weapon; the third, the jugular.

When the intruders were dead, two men entered from

the door, each holding a short blunt club. One of them whistled shrilly. The animals immediately left their victims and went to the men, lying down. All but one. The blood and excitement of the kill were too much to leave on command. His trainer went up to him and whistled again. The dog snarled, the short club cracked against the Doberman's skull.

Franks reached forward and turned off the TV monitor.

"What do you do with the bodies?" Sperry asked.

"Use them. Wrap them in canvas and dump them across town, where Delveccio runs his drug sales. The police will find them there and give Delveccio a hard time until he pays them off. Then the whole thing will be forgotten."

"But what about the people who sent them here?" Sperry asked. "They know."

Franks looked at him. "Who'll tell?"

Franks and Sperry went from the television control room to a luxurious office-apartment. Waiting for them was Mikhail Oleg, one of Franks' best pilots and an expert in electronic security systems. Oleg didn't look like a Russian fighter pilot; Oleg, with light brown hair and a sallow complexion, light body and soft voice, looked anything but Russian. Mikhail (Franks pronounced it Michael) Oleg had escaped from the Soviet Union in grand style. A fighter pilot with the Red air force, Oleg had gotten into a fight with another pilot. When it was over the other pilot was dead and Oleg was under arrest. Not for long. Considering years in prison and disgrace afterward, Oleg elected to go for broke. He killed an airport guard, slipped into his MIG-21 fighter, and took off. On his last gasp of fuel he emerged over mountain country in a rainstorm, saw a long concrete strip and dumped the MIG. He deliberately blew the tires to come to a stop before running off the end of the rain-slick runway. He was in northern Greece, and he'd landed at an old, abandoned war-time field.

The rest included some lucky coincidence and Sam Franks' policy of always paying well those in his employ. A Greek border patrol officer discovered the airplane and its pilot. Remembering a job he'd done for Sam Franks (through a code name) and the pay he'd received, the Greek got a message through to a number in Rome. He kept the MIG and its pilot hidden with the help of three of his soldiers, who saw in their reward for guarding their find and keeping quiet more money than they could manage from their pay in the next twenty years. The day after the phone call an old Boeing Stratofreighter landed at the remote airfield. The Boeing was slow and unwieldy but it could haul twenty tons of cargo and it could lift from the old airstrip.

Using maintenance manuals purchased from certain Egyptian officials, Sam Franks and a picked maintenance crew dismantled the wings and rolled the Russian fighter into the cavernous hold of the freighter. Mikhail Oleg, mystified by it all but with few alternatives, went along. At the Sardinian base he was put on ice while his story went through exhaustive scrutiny.

"Mike," according to Sam Franks, was one of the best things that ever happened to the organization. He was an excellent pilot, had been security officer for his wing, spoke several languages, and a death sentence was waiting for him back in Russia. In time, with every test behind him, he became a top-level confidant and an "officer" charged with control of major operations.

The three men sat down to an early dinner. Jonathan Sperry returned to his perpetual concern about discovery by any of the major governments, or Interpol finding them out. To Sperry, the strongest link in the organization, Sam Franks, was also potentially the weakest. Sam had been high in the command of the American strategic bomber force, and Sperry knew that no government casually dismissed the global whereabouts of a man informed about many of its major defense secrets.

"I mean"—Sperry pressed a point—"isn't it still possible they suspect you? Someone like you doesn't just disappear. If after a certain time you're not accounted for, and they become aware of our organization—especially after Butukama—isn't it natural they'd seek you out? The American computer system—and I'm familiar with it—"

To Sperry's surprise Franks agreed with him. "And the computer, any computer, is hard to satisfy. That's why

66

with Mike we made sure the Russians were sent back enough pieces of a wrecked airplane to convince them it was a MIG-21 that had crashed and exploded in the Greek mountains."

"Yes, of course," agreed Sperry, "but your case is different, Sam. You didn't crash, or anything like that. You just disappeared."

Franks shook his head. "As you know, I don't like explanations and I've told you from the first I was covered. Since then I don't believe you or anybody else in Pentronics has had reason to complain about my work or worry about my security. All right, now I'll give it all to you. Like you say, nobody disappears. I know the system. Anybody with SAC, or Tactical Air, or Navy, anybody in a command position with nukes, never disappears. If you're not accounted for you automatically go on a check-out list. That's why I happen to be in Australia."

"I thought this was Italy."

"But *I* am in Australia. In fact, I'm a pilot for Outback Airways. We fly Otters and Electras. We run cargo all through the bush to remote stations. I've been there for the past two years. My logbooks are up to date, I take a first-class physical every year, and I've vacationed three times, in Europe, South America, and Africa. My passport is in order, my taxes are paid. The computer, Mr. Sperry, is satisfied about the whereabouts and activities of one Sam Franks, ex-colonel, Strategic Air Command."

Sperry said nothing, waited uneasily.

"There's a man with my name who looks just like me—spitting image. Plastic surgery fixed details nature missed. He's a first-rate pilot, makes fifty thousand a year from an unknown source to keep his mouth shut and play his part. That's besides the twenty, thirty grand he knocks down as an airplane driver. It works out. Too bad he's going to have an accident."

"Accident?"

"This Butukama business isn't going to fade away overnight. The pressure's really going to be on us now. The computer will likely be programmed to spit up names of all people with nuclear weapons in their background. People will interview those names. Sam Franks will be one of them. They'll use experts. Most likely they'll drug him somehow—scope, I'd guess—and he'll come up with wrong answers. Or they might get his fingerprints and that would really blow it. So it's time for Sam Franks, ex-colonel and bush pilot, to crash and burn up. The computer will be fed the news. That will be the end of that. I wonder if I'm going to miss myself."

"It is all right, Sam," Oleg said. "I will attend your funeral if you'd like."

Sperry, obviously satisfied, shuffled through his briefcase. "Business, gentlemen."

"What about Kuto?" Oleg asked.

"He's right, John. I thought Hiroshi was supposed to be here," Franks said.

Sperry spread the papers out on the table. "We've had a change. Kuto thought it best for him to be on the scene. He's on the tanker right now. He's up to date on plans. If anything changes, we will radio Kuto aboard the tanker or carry out an airdrop with a message pouch."

"Okay," Franks told him. "Time still the same?"

"Ten days. We'll keep to the original schedule."

"Same course for the ship?"

Sperry tapped a paper. "The SS *Dorina*. Sailing time, course, speed—all of it. There could be changes, of course, due to loading delays or weather. But we can easily compensate and the information can be kept moving to Kuto at sea."

Franks turned to Mikhail Oleg. "What about the sub?"

"It is already at sea," the Russian said. "It remains submerged during the day. It surfaces at night every third day. It flies the French flag."

Franks turned again to Sperry. "John, what about confirmation of the cargo?"

Again Sperry pointed to a paper. "It's all right there. The Polish government is the major purchaser. They have told us that most of the jewels aboard that vessel were seized from their museums during the war by the Nazis. There has been no way for them to regain what they consider priceless national heirlooms."

"Their price?"

"Fifty million dollars. I will attend to collection and disbursement."

"Interesting," Franks said. "We destroy a city, and thousands of people, and we make eighteen million for the job. Here's a government that will pay nearly three times more for a bunch of damn trinkets."

"It only proves," Sperry said, "what we have always known. There's nothing cheaper than human life."

Franks looked up as Kali, the Arab, came in. Their meetings were never disturbed except for something of special importance. And if Kali himself were carrying the message . . .

"I am sorry to interrupt—" Kali began. Franks waved aside the apology. "A most unusual situation has arisen," the Arab said carefully. "Does the name of Steve Austin mean anything to you?"

"It means something if it's the same Austin I'm thinking of. Colonel Austin?"

"That is the one. The astronaut."

Franks glanced at the other men in the room. "Steve Austin. Crack test pilot. Big hero. Flew the last Apollo mission. Last man on the moon. He came back and got assigned to the shuttle test program. He was flying one of those bathtub killers when he piled it in. Tore him into pieces. The last I heard he'd lost his legs and an arm and there wasn't much left of him."

"You know this Austin?" Sperry asked.

"Not personally. I met him once but it was a long time ago, we were just two guys in blue suits." Franks looked at Kali. "What's it all about?"

Kali told the story as it had broken on the wire services. He went through the television interview and the subsequent wild fight, including how the two men, Austin and Schiller, both disappeared and then suddenly showed up at Kennedy International Airport.

"I suppose," Sperry said, "they hijacked an airliner?" He had the professional's contempt for amateur gestures.

"No, sir," Kali replied. "They got aboard an empty 707 waiting to be loaded. They captured or ejected the crew, started the airplane, and took off."

There had been a smile on Franks' face and it broadened with every new detail. "Where are they now?"

"No one knows that," Kali said. "But the latest report was that the airplane had a six-thousand-mile range, and was last seen flying over the Atlantic by two fighter pilots."

"Fighter pilots?" The question came from Mikhail Oleg, who was remembering his own escape and what would have happened to him if Russian fighters had ever caught up to him. "I do not understand. If fighters could intercept why didn't they shoot down the machine?"

"Because," Franks said, and grinned at him, "they don't do things like that in the States. You shoot down an intercontinental 707 and you've shot ten million dollars out of the sky. If those guys land and the news gets out where—and they *got* to land sooner or later—the airline figures it at least gets a chance to get back its property."

"But they are criminals and—"

"Money," Franks said. "It makes the world go round. Also, don't forget this guy *was* a hero." Then, to Kali: "Anything on position reports?"

"No, but we are trying to plot alternatives. Perhaps, Sam, the best way is for you to ask the question: If you were Colonel Austin, what would you do?"

"When you're under pressure, and you get time to think —and sitting in the driver's seat of a 707 all the way across the Atlantic is time to think—" Franks said quietly, "you reach out for the familiar, something you know about."

"Which would be?" Sperry asked.

"That airplane has enough range, with an hour's reserve, to get to central Libya. I know something about Austin's background. After his moon-flight publicity and crack-up, you'd have to have been on the moon to miss it. I'm sure I remember that when he was stationed in Europe his outfit used the Libyan desert for a gunnery range. Austin would remember those fields, and he'd remember that the runways were long enough to take the bird he's flying. I like it," he said suddenly. "We control those fields. Not directly, but that doesn't matter. What counts is my bet

Steve Austin goes for those fields. Kali, if I'm right, what would his E.T.A. be?"

"I'd say at least five hours."

"We can make it. We take the Sabreliner from here to Oristano. If the fighters are ready, and if my guess is right, we should be able to get a good intercept before he lands. I'd like to talk to that man before anybody else gets to him."

"Why?" Oleg asked.

"This man is famous all over the world. As the last man to walk on the moon. Also because he was mauled in a crash. They said he'd never walk again. According to what we've heard from Kali, he and another guy with no legs wrap up a bunch of people and steal an airliner. And now the two of them are flying it across the Atlantic. That's the kind of performance I like.

"There's something else I like about this Austin that's not public knowledge. Before he was an astronaut he was one of a few special pilots assigned to a killer strike force of F-111 fighter-bombers. Their mission was to take out every command post in Russia at the start of a war." He looked at Mikhail Oleg. "I saw that outfit in simulated action. And Austin, like everyone else in that outfit, had to be an expert in nuclear weapons. And that's *our* business." He tossed his cigar butt into an ashtray. "Let's move out."

"To me," Oleg said, "there seems to be too much publicity. Could it be this entire affair is a plant?"

"It could be. And you could be and I could be. And you know we'll check Austin and his friend out. But remember what happened to Austin. He lost both legs. And an arm. And an eye. And had his skull cracked open, ribs busted, and—he was more dead than alive. And you know what? Making a man like that into a special agent is asking just a little too much from any man, American *or* Russian."

Oleg did not reply.

"Look, Mike, why don't you see for yourself? I'll take Johnson with me in the F-4 and you can fly the MIG as top cover for us."

"It should be interesting," the Russian said.

71

CHAPTER 10

Sam Franks peered through the bubble visor of his helmet, studying the long brush of white painted against the dark blue sky. Franks was flying at 26,000 feet, lower than normal cruising altitude for the big F-4 fighter. The lesser height made possible his first glimpse of the contrail above him. Below was a solid undercast. Franks pressed his radio button.

"Tango to Sunflower."

Oleg's voice came back at once from his escort position well back to the right and slightly higher than the leading F-4. "I read you, Tango, I have them in sight."

"Right, Sunflower. I'll move up to their right so they can get a good look at us. You make your move from the left."

Oleg's voice came back, a bit tight, stiff. "As you say, Tango. I'm breaking now."

The MIG-21 was a flashing silver minnow. Oleg brought the gleaming fighter well below the big 707 at the same time Sam Franks slid the Phantom into formation with the jetliner. As soon as Franks confirmed by radio that the Americans in the 707 were aware of the Phantom, Oleg went to afterburner for a burst of speed, whipped beneath the 707, and came arcing up in a great climbing roll. Steve Austin and Marty Schiller had their first glimpse of the MIG as it arrowed before them and up to their right, the tailpipe ghostly orange flame and the fighter flick-responsive to the man at the controls. Oleg continued the roll, breaking out to the left, and when he snapped the airplane level it was locked precisely in place on the side of the 707 opposite Franks in the Phantom.

Schiller nudged Steve Austin. "If you're thinking what I'm thinking, someone out there is showing he knows what to do with that bird." Schiller stared past Steve at the MIG riding its invisible rail in the sky with them. "Russian fighter, isn't it?"

"MIG-21," confirmed Steve. "But it's got no markings. Looks like we've got a private party. Now look at the Phantom on your side, Marty. Israeli markings, but you can bet that's no Israeli fighter."

"Who?"

Steve shrugged. "All we know for sure is we've drawn more than flies. That's a Russian fighter on the left and an American fighter on the right, and they're obviously working together. They could scissors us without even breathing hard. And take another look. Each airplane has missiles *and* cannon. They—"

He cut off his own words as the Phantom slid in closer, handled beautifully, until its wing well overlapped the 707. Steve and Marty Schiller studied the front man in the cockpit as he signalled with his hand. He held up one finger, then two, then one, and finally both hands, one with all fingers and the thumb and the other with four fingers.

"I hope," Schiller said, "he flies as well with his feet as he did with his hands."

"They want to talk," Steve said. "That's the frequency signal he just gave us. One two one niner on VHF." Steve dialed the radio to the specified numbers and pressed his transmit button.

"Phantom, the Boeing here. Over."

Franks' voice came clearly into the earplug. "Roger that, Seattle. What's your fuel status?"

The words . . . no, the manner of speaking hit Steve. Whoever was in the Phantom, he was an American. The inflections of speech, the use of "Seattle" as a call sign . . . Seattle was where they built the 707 liners. An *American* . . . and a Russian fighter off to their left?

"Seattle, did you read Phantom?"

"Got you five by," Steve said. "Two hours at least. What's this all about?"

"Can't blame you, Seattle. I'll bet you and Schiller are just full of questions."

Steve and Schiller stared at each other. Questions were being answered before they were asked.

When the Phantom pilot called in again it was by name. "Austin, you can start your letdown now. Set up a thousand feet per. Hold your needle pegged at mach seven two. Got that?"

"Got it."

"Run it back, Seattle."

The other guy wasn't taking any chances. Steve eased off slightly on the power and fed in nosedown trim. "A grand a minute down at seven two, Phantom."

"Roger. We'll let you know any changes ahead of time. And, Seattle, no deviations from present course or those numbers without checking first."

Steel fist in the velvet glove. "What's home plate?" Steve said.

"Right where you were headed all the time. The strip due north of Goddua. Where you did your gunnery and bomb proficiency work when you were flying the Lead Sled. You'll be landing to the east. You've got twelve grand. Just like the old days."

Steve shook his head. "We know each other?"

"A long time ago we had the blue team in common . . . never mind, Austin. It can hold for later."

They know where we were going to land," Steve said. "Which tells us they've had an advance look at our scenario or—hopefully—it's just that our boy out there is an American or someone who's spent so much time with our people that—no, he's got to be an American and I'd bet once wore the blue suit—*and* that he once flew from Goddua like I did. He's heard about our exploits, put himself right into this seat with me and added it up. I also get the feeling this guy and I somewhere, sometime, crossed paths."

"Sounds like it, Steve. But what the hell is he doing in a Phantom with Israeli markings, which you say isn't an Israeli plane, and what is that MIG doing out there?"

74

"I'd say we may have a couple of big fish who've begun to take the bait. In case you've forgotten, that's us. I just hope we don't get swallowed whole—"

"Austin, we'll penetrate the cloud deck in a minute or so," came the voice from the Phantom. "The base is three grand above Goddua so hold your course until you break out. You'll find the strip dead ahead. Make a standard left pattern and go on in. The MIG will stay topside until we break through. I'll go back and well to your rear during penetration. Don't disappoint me, Austin."

"Wouldn't think of it," Steve said.

Mist whipped about the 707 as they slipped into the solid cloud deck. Steve let the autopilot take her down, choosing to sit back and monitor the ship. During the long descent through the grayness they heard nothing from the Phantom fighter, but Steve knew he sat well back of them, the radar specialist in the rear seat of the big F-4 holding them neatly on his scope. There wasn't anything they could do the Phantom couldn't do better. Besides, Goddua was their original destination anyway, and they were running low on fuel.

It looked like McKay would have good reason to be pleased with his scenario—however far-fetched it had once seemed. The people in the fighters had to be part of a pretty impressive operation. Just to get your hands on a MIG-21 or a Phantom you would need plenty of professional maintenance and a steady river of supply; you would need power systems and armament and skilled mechanics. And such an organization must have some ambitious operations. You could play all the games you wanted to with a small standard airplane whose parts and maintenance didn't mean much, but not with the highly intricate systems that went into fighters that cost three to four million dollars a crack.

They broke through the clouds three thousand feet above the ground. Far ahead of them, barely visible against the bleak sky and sand, bright orange smoke drifted before the wind. "I see them," Steve told Schiller as the latter pointed. The smoke gave him his wind direction and he set up the Boeing for the pattern and letdown. He waited until the last moment to drop the garbage. When the

75

gear, flaps, leading-edge flaps and spoilers all banged and rumbled into the airstream, the 707 was coming around tight, a huge fighter in the pattern, and Steve held her just right in a high-nosed flare, kicked thrust through the engines as he came over the threshold and put her down just as she stalled. The nosewheel slammed onto concrete and Steve was on the brakes, his hand hauling back the throttles to full reverse thrust. Light in weight, facing a brisk wind, the huge jetliner screamed to a stop within three thousand feet of touching down.

Thunder cracked overhead and Steve glanced up, hoping he'd be vindicated by what he expected to see. He was. The Phantom, standing on its wing, pitched out with razor precision.

"That was pretty, Austin," came the pilot's voice. "Take her straight ahead. A vehicle will lead you to the parking stand. Shut her down and wait for me there."

Steve went forward on the power as a truck with flashing lights pulled up before them, following the vehicle off the runway. A swarm of trucks assembled as he brought the jetliner to a stop and began shutting down all systems. Behind him Marty Schiller opened the main passenger door and a blast of hot air rushed into the cockpit. Steve glanced up from his check list and saw the Phantom turning off the runway. Overhead the MIG-21 was in the pattern with the gear down. Busy place, Steve thought.

He waited with Marty at the door, staring at a crowd of onlookers staring back at them. Beyond the still-growing crowd a truck raced toward them from the Phantom, now parked with the canopies open. The truck squealed to a halt, and Steve kept his eyes on the one man who held all his interest. The Phantom pilot left the truck, pushing his way through the crowd, and Steve had enough time to see the man as powerful, confident, probably long accustomed to command—the way he walked, the men making way for him . . .

Several men wheeled a stairway to the 707 and the pilot took the steps two at a time. He stood on the top platform, beefy fists on his hips, already staining his flight suit with perspiration. He nodded to Steve.

"You're Austin." A powerful hand shot out and Steve

clasped it with his own. "Mine's Sam." He examined Steve for a moment. "No two ways about it, we've met before. Your face was prettier then but what the hell"—he laughed —"so was mine at the time." He turned to Schiller. "And you're Marty Schiller. You're a big one, for sure. I saw the TV films, by the way. You two pretty much took over the communications satellites last night. Quite a party you had on that TV show. Okay, I know you're full of questions. Hang on to them for now and come with me."

The rapid-fire, one-sided dialogue left no chance for interruption. There was even less cause for argument. In Franks' eyes Steve and Schiller had fled their own land, in the process stealing ten million dollars worth of airplane, violating more rules and laws than they could count. They would know they could be shot on sight, beaten with impunity by the mob outside the airplane, or simply thrown into confinement. They would also know they were fair game to be held captive for any ransom offered by Pan American Airways or the American government or both. Perfectly natural, then, in fact inevitable, that they should go along with this man Sam whoever he was—especially since he at least appeared friendly. They had no options.

They climbed aboard the truck that had brought Sam to their airplane. For a moment they paused, watching the MIG-21 easing off the runway, trailing its drag chute. Crewmen ran to the Russian fighter. Steve was impressed. Whatever was going on at the old military strip where he had been based for thirty days at a time for gunnery and bombing training, it had snap to it. These people had the professional touch.

The truck took a long curving road along the base of a wide hill, and Steve was impressed by what he saw beyond the slope. There were at least a hundred planes in sight. Planes of all types and descriptions, everything from small twins to huge four-engine transports. He recognized cargo loaders, pipeline waiting to be loaded, stacked boxes of supplies and hangars sealed off for airconditioning. Nothing so unusual at first glance. Goddua was a large desert base for supporting pipeline and other operations. But that was at first glance. Steve also took in the unusually extensive electronics facilities. This place had every kind of radio antenna as well as elaborate radar facilities. And they were here with a Phantom and MIG-21. That added to unusual. The truck stopped beneath the wing of an ancient DC-4, a four-engined relic dating back to World War II but still used in boondocks country as an aged but reliable bird for almost any kind of odd-job flying. Their host climbed from the truck and motioned them aboard the old plane.

"Take those two seats there," he said. "We've got an hour's flight. Soon as we're off the ground, one of my men will bring you some dates and cold wine. Hold your questions until we're on the ground again. I'll have to ask you both to stay in your seats until we land."

They spoke only briefly during the flight of just under an hour. Steve and Schiller were busy trying to absorb what was happening to them. They were bone-tired—no sleep for over twenty-four hours that had involved the strenuous show in the television studio and the long flight across the Atlantic. Steve ate and drank hungrily, then, as he long ago had trained himself to do when he was tired and free of any immediate responsibility, he fell fast asleep.

He awoke as the DC-4 skimmed the end of a desert airstrip and settled gently to the ground. He and Schiller followed Sam's gestures, leaving the plane and walking through tortured air to a row of large tents. Steve needed only a moment to recognize that the tents were a sham, a façade for prefab structures inside. In the third tent down the row he found a large two-story structure, the bottom half forming a basement in the sand. The prefab structure trembled from powerful generators nearby. The rooms were airconditioned and surrounding them were rows of extensive communications equipment. Steve's expression went blank when he recognized a communications computer. Almost at the same moment their host reappeared from another room.

"You recognize the gear," he said to Steve. His words were a statement more than a question.

"Direct comsat link here. The computer"—he gestured —"you're running auto-transmit through the communications satellites." And to himself he thought that if this weren't McKay's jackpot target, it was a prime candidate. He only hoped he and Schiller wouldn't blow the hand.

"Good," Sam said. "Anything else?"

"You're apparently set up here as some kind of oil-drilling facility, or a pipeline company. That would explain the runway and tents, the antenna system too. To the outside world, anyway. And you're remote enough here so that no one from your other base, Goddua, can stumble inside and rattle your cage." He looked around him. "I might even wager you've got sweep radar in the end tent, which you don't need for pipeline or oil drilling. I'm not even sure you don't have your own comsat in orbit."

"You're a suspicious fellow, Austin. But you talk your mind. I tend to like that."

A jet cut low overhead, its sudden roar crashing through the building. "I think I know that sound," Steve said.

"Give it a shot."

"Well, the engines are used in a whole range of aircraft but only one of them sounds like—Gulfstream II."

A meaty hand banged his shoulder. "Hundred percent. Now let's move it."

They went outside and watched the big Grumman executive jet taxiing up to them. The crew kept the two engines screeching as they climbed into the airplane. They had only a moment to take in the luxurious interior before Sam motioned them to their seats. They sank into rich upholstery and fastened their belts as the Grumman turned at the end of the strip and went to full power.

They were passing through ten thousand feet before Sam threw off his belt and went forward. Steve exchanged glances with Schiller, who shrugged. Steve agreed with the unspoken message. Don't rock the boat.

Sam emerged from the front office with a smile on his face. He went past them with a trailing gesture for the two "guests" to move farther back into the cabin. Two flight attendants, both large and stocky men, and a single girl, unfolded a large table. Within moments the table was covered with a heavy cloth and the two men and the girl brought food to them.

Marty Schiller stared at a plate heaped with roast lamb,

vegetables, and a silver goblet frosty with chilled wine. "Mister, I don't know who you are," he said to Sam, "and when I find out, if I find out, I'd like to thank you for all this. Because if you got nothing else you got *style*."

Sam looked at him carefully.

They cruised at about 34,000 feet, Steve judged after an appraisal through the window. The air was satiny and there was hardly a tremble from the sleek Grumman.

During the next several hours as the Grumman flew north—a course Steve determined from the sun's position and glimpses of the African coast before darkness set across the earth far below—Steve went through a gentle sparring session with their apparent benefactor. Sam spoke only a few words during his meal. He ate stolidly, downing his food with long pulls at his wine. Finally he was finished, and three cigars appeared from his flight suit. Steve declined, but Marty accepted and soon wreathed himself in smoke. Sam's cigar pointed its glowing end at Steve.

"The Boeing. Why?"

Steve welcomed the chance, hoped he wouldn't sound too pat, or too offhand. He had to avoid over-explaining, rather let the other man fill in as many of the blanks as possible for himself—more plausible that way, less opportunity for Steve to louse himself up. "You mean stealing it?"

No answer. Steve shrugged and went on. "We'd gotten in way over our heads. Flying is something I know how to do. It looked like a fast way to split."

"It was that. Also a little sudden, wasn't it?"

"I don't know, it's strange, but in a way the whole thing seemed natural, like *déjà vu*, like it had already happened before. I guess I'd been building to this a long time without realizing it. That damn movie soldier and his big mouth just touched it off."

"What were your plans?"

"Not too many places to go with a hundred tons of airplane. Goddua seemed best. We thought it might be empty, and we were hoping the old field could still be used. Besides, those people aren't too fond of the people running our government, so it looked like our best bet. We

80

figured whoever got our plane in their hands could collect from Pan Am to get it back and might just be happy enough with the whole deal to send us on our way." He looked around the executive cabin. "But we sure didn't count on anything like *this*. Time for *your* explanations yet?"

Apparently not, because in answer Sam turned to Schiller. "What about you?"

"I go with him."

"So I notice. What else?"

"I teach famous cripples how to walk."

"You teach pretty good. You're also a big one," Sam said. "Hold up your hands, please." Marty brought his arms up, stretching. "Turn them," Sam added, then gestured for Schiller to lower his arms. The big man looked at Sam, waiting.

"And before you turned teacher?"

"Professional killer," Marty said.

"Special forces?"

"Twelve years as topkick. How'd you know?"

"Your wrists. Blue coloration. Comes from karate work, mainly. I've got three black belts. How good are you?"

"Very good."

Sam nodded to the two stocky men in the cabin with them. "Can you take them?"

"I'll give it a try."

Sam snapped orders in Arabic. In almost that same instant the guard closest to Schiller launched himself, hands extended. Marty came out of his chair with the fluid movement of a big cat. He did something with his arm and in an instant a knife gleamed in his hand. The guard twisted to avoid the blade as Schiller shouted. In that split second of attention to the knife, Schiller went forward with his head. The top of his skull smashed into the forehead of the guard, knocking him unconscious before he collapsed to the floor of the plane. By then the second man was on his way, stopping only at Sam's hasty command. In almost the same moment Schiller was back in his seat. The knife was gone.

"Where's the knife?" Sam demanded.

"Spring release in the forearm."

"Nice trick."

Schiller glanced at the guard sprawled on the floor, his forehead split open, bleeding profusely. The girl hurried to his side. "I'm sorry about that," Schiller said. "He looks like a good man."

"Forget it," Sam told him. "You taught him a good lesson. He's supposed to be the best. I'm curious, though. With your qualifications, how come you play teacher to a cripple?"

Steve wondered if he should take offense, decided not to. He knew enough already to recognize a test. And Marty was doing beautifully on his own.

To answer Sam, Schiller stood up slowly. "The trousers. Pull them up." He saw the wary look in the eyes of the other man. "No sweat. I stand still."

Sam leaned down from his seat to raise the trouser legs and reveal legs made of steel and bolts and nuts and plastic.

"Lost them in Nam" Schiller said. "Land mine." He waited until Sam resumed his seat, then went back to his own chair.

"What about the head?" Sam asked.

"Shrapnel. Chewed away the top of the head. Steel plate up there. Special cushioning. The top of the skull, just beneath the hair, is steel-knobbed."

"You're a real sweetheart." He studied both men. "In fact, the two of you make quite a pair."

"We may even get married someday," Steve told him.

Sam almost smiled. "You two got more tin between you than a sheet metal factory. Austin, here, he flies like he's got an angel up his tail. And you, Schiller, in a few seconds have just dumped a man who once killed seven—*seven*—men who hit him all at the same time. You two ought to rent out for bedtime stories. What are your plans now?" he asked them.

"That's pretty much in your hands, I'd say. The way it looks from here, it's your party. I mean," Steve said, "from what we've seen, the Phantom and the MIG, that old Charley Fifty-Four and this bird, the base facilities, that comsat tie-in beneth the tents . . . it looks to be quite a set-up."

"What about me?" Sam said. "You got any ideas?"

"SAC? For starters."

Sam chewed his lip. "Not bad. You can tell me more later. We're on the way in now. By the way, don't sweat about air piracy charges. It's been worked out. Libya has granted both of you political asylum. Your 707 is already on the way back to the States, flown by a picked crew, and is being returned undamaged to Pan American. You're off the hook—unless, of course, you're ever dumb enough to go back to the States."

"You're something else, Sam," Steve said.

"We aim to please. You ever get to Sardinia in your travels?"

"No."

"Take a look outside. You're about to discover it."

CHAPTER 11

Whatever they had seen at Goddua in the African desert was modest compared to the sprawling immensity of the base on Sardinia that spread before Steve this night —and not only was nothing hidden, full attention was being called to the presence of the huge installation.

They flew a wide pattern about the airfield, and Steve's practiced eye took in the long runways, the veinous spread of taxiways, the rows of hangars, and an incredible dispersion of supporting buildings and facilities. As they taxied from the runway Steve had full opportunity to see hangars capable of holding a Boeing 707 in their capacious interior. That meant enormous engineering, and he found himself looking for telltale signs. They were there, all brilliantly illuminated: power stations and substations, thick cabling, antenna, fuel farms, fleets of trucks and stations with crash vehicles, special buildings surrounded with barbed wire and armed guards, security police cruising the area . . . all elements of a huge base. Within a taxiing distance of about a mile Steve was able to make out the forms of several hundred airplanes.

Not even the night, broken as it was by hundreds of bright lights, could disguise the extraordinary number and diversity of airplanes. Fighters, bombers, transports, antisubmarine warfare planes, trainers, executive jets, old cargo ships. They taxied past a huge maintenance hangar, where Steve saw fighters with Italian markings, French markings, American, and with other insignia he couldn't identify.

He glanced ahead of their plane. An island of light pushed away the darkness and as they came closer he saw several hangars with floodlights around them—and row on row of jets, including at least twenty or more 707 and DC-8 models. Each hangar bore a huge sign that read PENTRONICS, INC.

They were *advertising?* This same outfit that had showed up out of nowhere with an American and a Russian fighter, that bounced along the desert in an old C-54, that concealed its modern computer-run communications beneath tents, that ran executive jets was now revealed in flood-lighted splendor. They couldn't be hiding anything —what they had here could be seen and photographed in detail not only by a high-flying reconnaissance snooper but by the Samos satellites as well. And you don't run up a towering electric bill trying to be inconspicuous.

He reviewed his conversations with Jackson McKay and Oscar Goldman . . . "It takes an organization to carry out what's happening. A big organization that reaches around the entire world. The key to their operations is the very nature of their organization."

This Pentronics outfit could actually be what they had been talking about only theoretically. An open operation.

84

You couldn't hide something this big, and why bother? Out there, rolling past them as they taxied, was an operation known throughout all of Europe and the rest of the world, for that matter. Pentronics was the outfit that had cornered the bulk of maintenance, overhaul, repair and modification to the air fleets of NATO.

The Grumman parked in front of an operations building, and they found a station wagon waiting for them. Standing for a moment on the outside step, Steve made out at a distance, in a compound isolated from other activity on the field, several English Electric Lightnings— among the best fighters turned out for the Royal Air Force—all of them with missile armament, as if on combat alert.

The variety of aircraft and their national origins seemed appropriate for an organization that did much of NATO's modification and overhaul work. Likewise for just about everything else, including ground security. But not so for interceptors on combat alert. Steve would have offered odds those Lightnings were not flown by RAF pilots, nor had anything to do with the RAF.

All about him sprawled an enormous organization. But it was public knowledge. It was known to the NATO governments. Obviously it was also well known to the Russians and their allies as well. No secret outlaw operation there.

But what if you functioned as an organization within an organization? An international criminal organization at home inside and behind a known legitimate one.

You needed jet fighters. Pentronics dealt with hundreds of jet fighters, and who was to stand around counting noses? You needed huge jet transports. Okay, the field was filled with them, and you couldn't tell what was inside an airplane by looking at it parked on the ramp. You needed an operational system through the main airways and byways of the world. Excellent. Pentronics was the parent outfit, and within or at least under the control of Pentronics you had subsidiary organizations that dealt with cargo and charter flights, with aerial survey work, with pipeline and other activity, with photography and rental and special service operations.

And the best way to keep something secret is to wave it under the noses of everyone looking for it so hard they'll never see what they're looking for.

Steve in a brief glance had already seen enough to paint much of the picture (of course, he knew enough to look for it). The MIG-21 and the Phantom, the activity in the desert, the swift flight to this base on Sardinia, and above all, the obvious strength and command of Sam . . . Steve knew that McKay and Goldman would have liked to have seen for themselves. But they would also have been pleased things were beginning to shape up as planned.

As for himself, from here in it would be freelance, move with the tide, until . . . He went with Marty and Sam into the vehicle waiting by the airplane. They drove quickly along a winding road columned with trees. He almost laughed to himself, realizing he suspected even tree trunks and branches, especially if artificial, of housing surveillance systems, including closed-circuit television, as well as means of stopping any vehicle dead in its tracks—an unobtrusive security web.

They drove through a high archway into a courtyard framed by thick concrete walls. Steel gates closed behind them. A tall dark man in a business suit was waiting for them. Steve caught the name Kali in the brief exchange between Sam and the stranger. He judged him to be an Arab, or from somewhere in the Mediterranean area. The building they entered was solid as a fortress, essentially a steel-and-concrete cube. From the look of air and exhaust systems Steve suspected he was in the equivalent of an iceberg, with only the tip of the building visible to the eye. They walked along several corridors, went through doors of thick bulletproof glass, were checked by unseen observers and electronic systems.

Finally they entered a luxuriously appointed apartment. The tall Arab (if that's what he was) left. Sam went to a bar, asked their choice, poured drinks. Steve glanced at the expansive living room, noted that it had no windows. Sam took a long pull at straight Scotch, motioned them to seats. No more preliminaries now.

"We've been checking you out," he said. "We need

good men. You two seem to fit, each in your own way. Interested?"

"That . . . that depends," Steve said slowly. Slowly? He could hardly talk. He turned his head to Schiller and found the movement required enormous effort. What the hell? Were their drinks drugged? He found himself staring at Marty, beginning to speak, but the words seemed impossibly heavy, refused to come past his lips.

"Don't try to talk"—the sound came from an impossible distance. "If you think you've been given a drug, you're right. I'm amazed you're still conscious. The drug, by the way, isn't in your drink. It's a gas and I've been immunized against it. Your friend is out cold. The drug is harmless. In about two hours it will wear off. You should . . ."

The words began to echo until they became a jangling reverberation. His eyesight began to fade. It all seemed familiar. Like pulling too many g's in a fighter. Or a centrifuge. The instructor's explanation at the time . . . Blood drains away from the head. Eyes need blood the most, gray out when blood begins to drain away . . . You can black out while you're still conscious, you're awake but without blood and oxygen to the eyes they lose vision . . . And he had only one eye and it was all very damned familiar. He was paralysed. Like pulling all those g's in the tank going around and around. The gray was going darker when he saw a door open across the room. Figures in white moved into his line of vision, wavered and then melted into a single blob of whiteness that swiftly darkened and—

CHAPTER 12

He lay quietly, eyes closed, not moving. He was strapped down, legs, arms, midsection. He put some strain into his neck. Locked solid. He thought of using the extraordinary strength of his bionics legs and left arm to tear loose. What good would it do?

None, except to demonstrate his own stupidity. He doubted if they'd caught on to the unusual power harnessed in his body. Why waste what might be a critical advantage? He opened his eyes, eye . . . even if it seems to be two eyes . . . stared straight ahead. Side vision was limited because of the head restraints to what was visible by moving his eye within the confines of its socket.

He saw men and women in white hospital gowns. Strapped down, a bright light directly overhead, figures in hospital gowns—examining room. Cool air across his body. He was naked.

A man's face moved closer, directly in front of and above him, compensating for his restricted head movement. And one eye. This fellow was considerate. A doctor of some sort. They had been studying or examining him, Steve knew. A neat way to put someone out. He must compliment Sam on that. Gas, odorless and tasteless and invisible. Temporary block in the nervous system. No aftereffects, no struggle.

"My neck is killing me," Steve said. The doctor nodded.

Moments later the restraints were gone and a sheet was placed over him. Steve moved his head from side to side. He was stiff and sore. "How long have I been on here?"

"Two hours, Colonel Austin. You're amazing. We knew about your accident, of course. And since your escapades in television we did as much research as we could. Not much, I'm afraid. But when you were brought in here we did a thorough examination—direct probing, fluoroscope X rays. We'll probably frame the X rays."

Well, they didn't know as much as they thought they did, which was a good thing. The servomotors in his legs and his arm; they knew about those. But there was a world of difference between servomotors to produce so-called normal responses and strength and the systems that made up the cyborg Steve had been transformed into. If they suspected his true capabilities, well, these straps would never have been released. They'd probably have used steel bands.

"Where's my friend?" Steve asked. "Marty Schiller."

"Safe," replied the doctor.

"That's not saying *where*," Steve pressed. He wondered how far this could go, how much clout he might have because of Sam's strong interest in him.

"Mr. Schiller has also undergone an examination. He is in another room, much like this one. He is in no way harmed."

Steve had no choice but to settle for that now. Time enough for the hero routine when and if it ever became necessary.

"Would you mind some questions, Colonel Austin?" Then, quickly, the doctor added: "Professional questions."

Steve knew that what he said would be used in the evaluation Sam had set up on him. So far he'd managed to keep to himself his tremendous strength and speed, the unique capabilities he enjoyed as a cybernetic organism. Only Marty Schiller was aware of his powers. Still, he knew he could slip in what he said to this doctor or anyone else probing in the area of his medical, bionics and related modifications. If he told everything *except* his overwhelming strength and related superiority to the average person, he could keep matters as they were.

So he discussed the Hufnagel valve that had saved and improved his heart system. There was much discussion about the special ribs, the artificial bone and cartilage, the plate in his skull that provided additional cushioning for his brain. The system of modification to nerve, muscle, tendon, sinew and bone endings where they had been severed, and their subsequent connection to the bionics limbs. It all had to fit what they had learned through their meticulous examination of his body while he lay unconscious. This exchange, as well as Steve's demonstrated ability with the 707 as witnessed by Sam, to say nothing of his background as a test pilot, fighter pilot and astronaut —well, Steve guessed he'd come wrapped in the right package to induce Sam to buy.

"By the way," Steve said, "where's Sam?"

"Sam? I didn't realize you two—well, I imagine Colonel Franks will be here any moment."

Steve nodded. *Colonel Sam Franks. So that's who he was!* Put together, it was a name Steve knew, and now it was all coming back in a rush. Not that he remembered meeting the man. There had been so many in uniform. But he remembered what had happened to Colonel Samuel A. Franks. Crack pilot in the Strategic Air Command. One of the best—tough, natural leader, headed for general's rank. And what he did with old B-52s out of Thailand against North Vietnam was rewriting the rule books of air war. He was a genius at tactics and electronic countermeasures. He hit targets in North Nam without losing a ship. In late 1972 and the first days of 1973 Nixon had sent the big bombers in against Hanoi and Haiphong. Franks had led in many of those planes.

But something was different this time. The B-52s were going in along the same routes, again and again. Missiles began finding their targets and B-52s started going down. Before he knew what was happening Franks saw ten percent of his entire bomber fleet blown out of the air. He did everything possible to stop the slaughter. He screamed to Washington to change the routes, let him use the old B-29 tactics developed against Japan back in the "big war." He wanted to put an umbrella of fighters over the B-52s and go in on the deck with heavy loads. The Pentagon nixed it, the losses climbed.

Franks was up one night in a formation of six bombers.

The SAM missiles bracketed them—and Franks raged as five huge B-52s went down. He blew his top and shoved the nose of that 200-ton airplane down, pushing her right to the wall, and he kept going down faster and faster, the North Vietnamese gunners believing all the time they'd scored a hit on his plane as well.

Franks pulled out just over the trees in a wild flight that scared his crew more than the missiles had ever done. He went over Hanoi at rooftop level, the airplane sounding like a wave of thunder. He dropped bombs in a long string. When he hit the coast he went even lower, stunning the defenses. He didn't go straight home. He made a rush for Haiphong, and when he hit *that* town, he dumped the rest of his bombs along the harbor. A big Russian freighter lifted out of the water, broke in two, sank.

They cashiered Sam Franks. They did it rough. Sam knew he was a sacrifice to the gods of new diplomacy, but that didn't make it easier to take. He disappeared from sight.

And here he is, thought Steve, working out his bitterness. Except by now it had to be cold, hard hate . . .

Almost on cue with the end of his mental run-through, Sam Franks came into the room. He nodded to the doctor. Steve sat up on the table and the doctor handed him a robe as another man entered the room and came up to Franks. About five feet ten, slight build, fair complexion. Seemed to wear a brooding expression, gave off a mixture of suspicion and self-confidence.

"Howgozit?" Sam asked. Even the everyday expressions of Sam Franks told of his background. Pilots used the "Howgozit" charts for a running record of squawks about their airplanes. Now that he was looking for clues about Sam's background, they almost seemed to leap at him.

"I'm fine. Now," Steve said, looping the robe belt about his middle. "But if you have any more fun and games scheduled, try telling me first, will you? You might find out I'd be willing to co-operate with someone who's saved my bacon the way you have so far."

Sam nodded, led them from the medical room down a long corridor to the apartment where he'd been sent into dreamland. Sam pointed to a bedroom door. "That's yours, Austin. You'll find a flight suit your size in there. Your boots have been repaired. Your personal things are on the dresser. In a couple of hours a minimum wardrobe will be ready for you. Anything else you want comes later. We'll wait for you here."

He changed quickly. He hated the feel of a hospital robe; nothing ever felt better on him than a flight suit. He found his watch and personal belongings. His boots had been repaired and shined to high gloss. What had Sam said? A minimum wardrobe had been prepared for him. More to come later. Okay, he was being told things, such as that he'd been accepted. He went into the other room, stopped short at the sight of Marty Schiller. "You all right?" he said quickly.

"Yeah." Too terse for Marty.

"But two of my best people aren't," Sam Franks broke in. He didn't seem angry. "Schiller broke two of the straps on his table. With his hands." He looked at Schiller. "You could have done something stupid after that, but you didn't. I like that."

"I thought," Steve said, "you said something about two of your people—"

"Schiller tore his straps in half with his hands. Some of the people in the room objected, tried to stop him. A couple of lumps and bruises, maybe a broken bone or two.

"Now, would you mind taking seats over there? What happened earlier today won't be repeated. It was necessary, but now you've even passed the X rays. You're both home free."

Marty Schiller was still tense. "Who's Pretty Boy?" he asked, jerking a thumb at the still-silent stranger with them.

The man was on his feet, face flushed, eyes angry.

"This," Sam continued, "is Mike Oleg. One of the best pilots I've ever known. He's been with us for two years."

Oleg stared at them, his features blank.

"Not too friendly, is he?" Steve said.

"Let's say he's a little shy. Likes his privacy. Also, he's not paid to be friendly. Well, Austin, how do you add it up?"

Steve took his time, wanting to sound plausible—not too informed but open about everything he'd seen and could reasonably, with his background, be expected knowledgeably to speculate about. He said certain things were obvious, and it all started with the sight of the MIG-21 and the Phantom in the same sky with the Boeing 707. When he was through he had given an accurate outline of the organization. "The way it looks to add up." he said, "you've almost surely got to have links around the world in all sorts of industrial, shipping, political and military areas. I don't see how you could operate on your scale if you didn't." He put in everything except the conviction he now had that Pentronics was locked in, beyond question, with the international marketing and use of nuclear weapons. Let that come from Sam Franks.

Sam had turned to Marty Schiller. "Want to add anything?"

"Sure. How much do you pay?"

"You seem pretty sure of yourself."

"Bilge. You've had us on the red carpet, the grill and the red carpet again. You showed us things. You know our background and our capabilities and you're interested. It's this way. An outfit like yours needs the best people. We're the best. You're going to make us an offer. And seeing that at the moment we're what they call at liberty, you figure we're going to accept."

"Okay," Sam told them. "Time to wrap it up. We want you to join our outfit. In your own case, Austin, you're a great pilot. But I've got pilots coming out my ears, any size or shape or language. Pilots are for sale—cheap. But people with your experience—and we've even got some use for your name and who you are—that's different.

"Part of what I'm saying is that with some men a word or handshake is commitment. I think you two are like that. We've all committed before, did what we were supposed to do, walked away when there was nothing else left.

"We're down to it, Austin. You want in?"

"Yes, but suppose I said no?"

"You'd have proved me a bad judge of men—which could ruin my self-confidence. By the way, speaking of judging men"—he gestured to Oleg—"don't be put off by

Mike. Like I said, he's not too chummy but that's just his way." He paused. "A hundred grand a year to start. The cash is deposited to your account in any bank and country you want. To hell with the details. That can all come later."

"Your friend, here," Steve said, pointing to Oleg. "I assume that's where your MIG-21 came from. But what brought *him* to you?"

"He killed a man. Under the wrong conditions."

Oleg said nothing.

"He killed a man with his hands. His own neck was on the block. Mike took off. It's a long story but we got him and his machine. He joined us. Like I said, he's one of the best. Anything else about Mike?"

Steve shook his head.

"Matter of fact," Franks said, "I was in the same boat."

He left it there, but Steve couldn't help thinking how literally right Franks was. He was in the same boat because he'd blown up the wrong boat—at least for that moment in the impersonal game of international politics. Socking it to a Russian boat was a distinct no-no when Sam Franks did it. Off with his head.

"All right then. You'll move quickly into a command position on my level. You'll meet the few other principals as fast as you do.

"It's an old story, Colonel. We're back in the death business. But you're no stranger to that. You were in that one-eleven outfit that was set to toss a bundle of thermonukes into the Soviets' front yard if the word came."

"If. A big word, Sam. What's your point?"

"It's all part of getting clued in on how you'll act. We want to know as much as possible about how you and Schiller will take to the heat. We still need to know more. Only now the time for dry runs is over. No more simulated exercises.

"Let's go for a little action."

CHAPTER 13

They flew the first leg of their mission from Sardinia to Ubrique in southern Spain. Not to the city itself, but to an airfield nestled within steep hills and mountains, isolated from neighboring communities. Sam Franks flew right seat, concerning himself with operational procedures, leaving Steve to handle the big Nord. The airplane was new to Austin. She was thick-bellied and wide-winged with four powerful turboprops. "Not much in the speed department," Franks had told him, "but it can show even the C-130 a couple of tricks in getting in and out of tight fields. We'll be flying just below gross. Much of the load is fuel including a cargo compartment tank, so stay close to your CG and load limits."

No real need to sweat the Nord, Steve found. He'd flown the C-130 many times, and this ship had everything going for it, including a lighter touch on the controls. He needed that touch as Sam talked him into the isolated strip. "We're about fifty miles north of Ubrique," Sam directed. "Take up a heading of two zero zero and hold nine thousand until I tell you to start down."

Steve flew her on the money, holding course and altitude, and wondering where Marty Schiller was—where, in fact, he had been the last several days. He'd thought it best not to ask yet, but he was getting damn curious—edgy.

"We're a couple of miles out," Sam said. "Get ready to dump her in, Austin, and I mean *dump*. Balls to the wall."

"Say the word."

Franks waited until a panel light blinked at him. "Okay, we're in position and we've got clearance. Dump."

Steve dumped. Gear down, full flaps down, leading edge flaps extended, spoilers chewing up the lift on the wing, the props flat. The Nord came out of the sky like a goose with crumpled wings, and finger-responsive all the way. Steve held her in the crazy descent until the last possible moment, tapped power and put her down on all three, slamming in prop reverse a good hundred feet from the edge of the runway. They crashed to a halt in a cloud of red dust, the ears ringing. Sam tapped him on the shoulder. "Very nice. Just what I needed for my sinuses."

They rolled back to the end of the runway. A Spanish air force officer climbed aboard, spoke briefly to Sam, who scrawled his signature on a clipboard. Exactly twelve minutes later they were ready. Steve fired up the engines and waited for the word from Sam.

"Take her out under max and hang her on the props to six grand. Two one five's your heading."

The seven passengers in the airplane, already shaken by the falling descent and crash-slam landing, went completely white during the take-off and climb-out. Even Sam ended up gripping his seat armrests as Steve took the Nord away from the ground in a precipitous upward lunge, holding up the nose in a drastic angle, just above the edge of a stall. At six thousand he eased her into level flight and fingered the throttles to cruise, holding a course of 215 degrees steady. The Atlantic spread forever before them.

Sam called back for coffee, handed Steve a mug. He lit a cigar, threw off his seat belt and leaned closer to Steve. "We're interested in an ocean liner. SS *Dorina*. About sixteen thousand tons."

"How far out?"

"Three hundred twenty miles. About two hundred people aboard, including crew, which doesn't interest us. The cargo does."

"Does Swami tell all or do we play guessing games?"

"The *Dorina* is carrying something like a quarter billion dollars worth of jewelry. I wouldn't pay you a dime for the stuff myself, but the Polish government feels different."

Steve waited for more.

"Their contact told us that there's no real value on the goods. He says most of it was confiscated during the war by the Nazis and Poland has never been able to get it back. The stuff is headed for the States, where it's supposed to be broken up and sold to private collectors. If that happens, and the Poles are afraid it will, they say there's no way they'll ever get back the crowns and scepters and whatever else marks their national history. So they're desperate patriots. And desperate anything pay through the nose."

"How desperate in this case?"

"Fifty million."

"Fifty million?"

"If we deliver the goods in their front yard. Nowhere else. If we make partial delivery, miss some of their stuff, they'll scale down payment. It's a good deal." Franks finished his coffee and tapped ashes into the mug. "It's a good beginning for you, Austin."

"What if someone objects to your making off with their jewelry?"

"You use good business practice, Austin. Good business practice is to insure that no one objects, which brings us to a couple of items I've waited until now to tell you. About thirty miles from the *Dorina* is something that looks like a big tanker. We should be able to home in on it any moment."

"It's not a tanker," Steve said drily.

"Right. No oil aboard."

"You've put something together on the order of the old Q-ships?"

Franks laughed. "Right again. The old Q-ships, as you know, were merchantmen with guns hidden behind false panels. Like I said, there's no oil aboard this tanker. Plenty of oil lines on the deck, but they're false and they drop flush into the deck when someone pushes a button."

"Which gives you a landing deck."

"And inside, that tanker is a complete helicopter base. Elevators, maintenance, the works. There's plenty of fuel, though. The kind the choppers and this bird we're flying use."

"We land on your glorified tub."

"Which is also our refueling base away from home."

"It should be interesting. How long is the deck?"

"Six hundred fifty feet, no-obstruction approach."

"That's cutting it thin, Sam. Very thin."

"Not really. The tanker can do better than twenty knots. The surface wind's about eighteen. That gives you thirty-eight knots for free. If you can't hack it, Austin, I'll eat this damned airplane."

"I'm inspired by your confidence."

"We also have a sub in the area. A German snorkel from the war us old guys fought in. Nearly thirty knots submerged. Right now she's there just in case Murphy gets into the act."

"That I recognize," Steve said. "Murphy's Three Laws of Physics. And the first law is that whatever can go wrong, will go wrong."

"Second law says that whatever's wrong is bound to get worse," added Franks.

"And the third law is that when the first two laws have been passed and you're still around, panic."

"We think alike," Franks said, pleased. "One more surprise for you. Your friend's aboard the tanker."

"Marty?" At least his question about Marty's absence was now answered without his having had to ask.

"None other. He's back in his element. He's got eight professional tough guys under him. They go aboard the *Dorina*."

He went silent. Worried, Steve searched the ocean for the ships.

Steve understood quickly how Sam Franks had earned his reputation in the Strategic Air Command. The moment the ships drifted into sight Franks shifted gears into computerlike efficiency, no easy conversation, no banter. He seemed to take on new strength, authority.

Steve set up a wide orbit that placed the tanker between the Nord and the distant SS *Dorina*. On his headset he heard his radioman talking with the tanker. One name was repeated several times: Kuto. Steve filed it away for future reference. Using binoculars he watched elevators rising along the sides of the tanker. Four large helicopters were rolled onto the deck, and the engines started.

A man came into the cockpit with them. "They're jammed, Colonel," he said to Franks, who nodded. "The full frequency?"

"Yes, sir. Anything they try to send will be hash. We have all their main and standby freqs, Colonel. We've got them covered like a blanket."

Franks turned to Steve. "Take her down to a thousand and give me a pattern around the liner."

Steve nodded. "Down to a grand and circle. Right."

As he descended in a wide curving line he saw three helicopters leave the tanker. He recognized them as they swung in the direction of the liner. British-made Sikorskys. Westlands, if he remembered right. Husky machines. He wondered what they were up to.

At a thousand feet he leveled off and started the wide pattern, his left wing lowered and pointed toward the ship. The helicopters slipped beneath them, moving into a formation leading the *Dorina*. Steve couldn't figure it. Each chopper flew just ahead of the liner, one directly before the ship, the others in line-abreast formation. They held their position for five minutes, then eased away. One flew to the right and ahead of the *Dorina*, the others well to the side of the ship.

Steve was crossing over one of the choppers when he noticed the liner swinging into a wide curve. As he watched the ship tightened its turn more and more until it was heeled over, continuing the turn. It ran in that same inexplicable fashion for ten minutes. What the hell was the matter with them down there, Steve wondered. They act like everyone in the ship is—the thought sent a cold wave down his spine—dead. He had to force the thought to mind. And out of it.

He glanced at Franks, who was studying his watch. Franks switched his microphone to transmit. "Tangerine to Outlaw One, you read?"

"One here. Five by."

"Everybody suited up, One?"

"That's affirmative, Tangerine."

"Two and Three, you people copying?"

"Two here. Affirm."

"Three copies."

"Okay. One, you go in according to plan. Two and Three, flank them from each side just in case. One, keep me informed. Let's hear it."

Each helicopter confirmed the call. Two choppers slid in to flank positions, and Steve saw machine guns directed toward the ocean liner from the helicopter cabins. The third machine, Outlaw One, made a beautiful curving approach to the still-circling ship. It was no cinch, Steve knew, because of the *Dornia's* speed and the winds buffeting off her structure. As he watched, the chopper moved directly over the stern, hovering above a recreation area. Until this moment Steve hadn't made out the bodies sprawled along the deck. None moved.

The helicopter hovered low, rocking in the winds. Rope ladders went out and black-clad forms climbed quickly to the deck. The men worked swiftly, dragging aside bodies and furniture, and Steve watched the chopper fight her way in to a landing.

"One to Tangerine. We're down. Nothing's moving here."

"Get your people onto the bridge," Franks ordered. "Put that thing back on course and lower speed to ten knots."

"One standing by." The black-suited figures ran forward. Several minutes later the *Dorina* eased from her uncontrolled circle, took up her former course, and reduced speed.

"Outlaw One, let's get with it," Franks said into his mike. "Status report."

"Roger, Tangerine. Nothing's moving anywhere our people can see. We've got them below decks now."

"Let me know as soon as you find the goods."

"One out."

Steve looked at Franks. "What the hell is going on down there?"

"Except for the people who landed in that chopper, everyone aboard that ship is dead. Dead people don't send messages for help. They don't fight. They don't even interfere. We want what that ship is carrying. There's a small army—was a small army—guarding that cargo. If we tried to take what we wanted by force I doubt if we could have handled it without tearing up the ship and losing a lot of our own people. And end up with the *Dorina* screaming to the whole world for help."

"*How,* in God's name, did you manage to kill everyone aboard that ship?"

Franks smiled. It was an expression Steve hadn't yet seen on his face. He could do without seeing it again. "Nerve gas," Sam said after a pause.

"Nerve—" Steve shook his head. "Where the hell did you get that?"

"Where? We bought it."

"You say it like you went to some market and found it waiting for you."

"Just about," Franks told him. "We bought it from the American army in Germany. There's a major in a chemical warfare outfit who keeps the records for his division. He likes the good things in life. All he had to do was alter some records. We helped him. We've got experts in that line. He got three hundred thousand in a numbered account in Switzerland and we got six tons of Green Ring Four. I see you recognize the brand name."

Steve's knuckles were white on the control yoke. "I recognize it. It's worse than the Tabun the Germans manufactured in the Second World War."

"Right. It's odorless, it has no taste, no effect on the lungs and skin, and just a whiff kills by paralyzing the body and the brain. Takes about thirty seconds. We figured ten minutes for the stuff the choppers sprayed behind them so it could get into the ventilation systems and be distributed throughout the ship."

"Look, Sam, that's a hell of a—"

"Austin, keep something in mind, and I'm being patient because this is your first operation with me. Remember we didn't produce that gas. Our government, that's who produced it, and shipped it to Europe, and around the rest of the world, keeping it ready to use against people anywhere, everywhere. And it was an American officer who sold it—and his lousy soul—for money. *He* sold it and *he* sold out. We were simply the customer. Remember one more thing. If you had to go, *Colonel,* what would be your choice? Nerve gas that puts you under with a single good whiff of the stuff, or the napalm dropped in Nam?"

Franks studied the ship through binoculars, leaving Steve a chance to try to control the churning knots in his stomach. The way this man rationalized . . . My God, you just didn't . . .

"You know, with Green Ring Four a gas mask is worthless." Franks spoke as if he had no connection with the silent mass slaughter below them. "We found out the armed guard for the jewels we're after had masks. They counted on them, too. Didn't do them much good. You need an impermeable suit and a closed recycling system. But I hardly need tell *you* about pressure suits. Score one for spinoff from the space program."

He pointed ahead of the transport. "See that? We knew we should be running into a front about here. Just what the doctor ordered. Take her down to five hundred, Austin."

Steve started the descent. Ahead of them the sky was gray and heavy with clouds. Isolated showers presaged the beginning of a solid front. In another twenty minutes they'd be in it. "Look over to our right," he heard Franks say. Steve saw a big Russian cargo helicopter chopping low over the water. "Mike Oleg's at the controls. I told you he was good. He has to be to get that thing down on the ship. He won't have more than a foot or two to spare with those rotors."

The chopper on the deck was already moving with the ship, well off to the side. Franks was right; Oleg was damned good. He slid the big helicopter onto the *Dorina* as though he were berthing a small ship with knifeblade precision.

"Okay, Austin, take this thing over to the tanker and put her down. I'll call in and set it up. She'll head directly into the wind for us."

Steve blanked his mind of everything but the flying. As good as Oleg was with the helicopter, he'd have to be even better with the Nord. Oleg could always back off from a poor approach. Once Steve committed to landing, that was

102

it. But the Nord handled beautifully and he had that bonus of thirty-eight knots of wind force. He surprised himself when he slammed to the deck and came to a full stop with a third of the metal plating still stretched out in front of him. "Back her up," Franks ordered. "Take it slow and easy. Watch the man to your left for signals."

Steve nodded, kept on brake pressure and eased the props back into the reverse thrust he'd used for landing. The Nord backed up slowly, easing to the very end of the deck. "Okay, hold it there," Franks said. Moments later the Nord was cable-secured to the deck. "Shut her down and let's move out."

A helicopter had dropped to the tanker deck. Several men stood by the doorway waiting as Steve and Franks put on impermeable suits and globe helmets. They checked out the pressure and snorkel exhaust valves and climbed aboard the helicopter. "Always chance of gas residue," Franks explained by suit radio. "Nasty stuff, as you know. We don't want even a whiff. Could screw up your whole life."

They made the trip to the *Dorina* quickly, the helicopter hovering over a cleared space just behind the bow. They went down by rope ladder. Two men in the sealed suits, automatic rifles at the ready, waited for them.

Steve felt as if he were moving in a slow-motion nightmare as they went through the ship. Bodies were sprawled grotesquely almost everywhere they looked, collapsed wherever they happened to be when the nerve gas invaded their systems. There was little sign of any violence or suffering. Steve felt as though he were walking through a museum of wax figures.

They watched as suited men carried heavy metal cases toward the waiting cargo helicopter on the ship's stern. "That's what we came for," Franks said.

They watched several men carrying large sacks. "The men on these jobs are allowed to take whatever cash they can find. That means from the bodies, the staterooms, especially the ship's safe," Franks said. "Nothing else. No personal jewelry or belongings. You can trace those, but not cash. It's a sort of added bonus for them."

Numb, beyond words, Steve followed Franks to the

bridge where they ran into four men with automatic weapons. Steve froze when he recognized Marty Schiller through his helmet. Marty somehow waved to him, and Steve managed what he hoped was a friendly gesture.

The rest was a blur as they worked their way forward, the helicopter coming down to a low hover as they climbed up the rope ladder. Moments later they were on their way back to the tanker. Steve was startled to realize the sky had turned a dark, angry gray and that rain fell heavily about them.

They stepped from the helicopter to the steel deck. "Walk over there," Franks said, pointing to a yellow circle on the deck. A boom arm swung in from the side of the ship. "Hang on to that railing," Franks ordered. They gripped a metal rail as chemicals were sprayed across, over and beneath the suits. "Okay, this way," Franks said. They went through another shower, this time with sea water, and were helped from their suits. Franks wanted them back on the Nord as quickly as possible, and Steve found the transport fueled and ready.

He did everything with numbed body and mind, starting the engines, running through the check list as the tanker turned back into the wind and went to full speed. By now the surface winds were almost gale force, and the Nord rushed into the air with room to spare. Following orders from Franks, he circled around both vessels as the helicopters returned to the tanker. With the choppers safely aboard and sent below decks, the tanker moved away from the Dorina under full speed.

"Chestnut to Tangerine. Come in, please."

The voice cut through Steve's numbness. Japanese accent, unmistakable. He listened as Franks replied.

"Tangerine here. Go ahead."

"You are very clear? Everything has been accomplished. There will be no need for further contact."

Franks let nothing interfere with business. "Roger that, Chestnut. Tangerine out."

He turned to Steve. "Keep the Dorina in sight. We got about twenty minutes to go."

Twenty minutes to what? Steve didn't want to know. He was grateful for the worsening weather and the need to devote his full attention to fighting the growing turbulence. The Nord rocked and trembled in gusts, and Steve made himself a part of the airplane. By the time the twenty minutes had passed he could barely make out the ship below them. He heard a voice on intercom from the cabin behind them. "It's all set, Colonel."

"Right," Franks replied. "Stand by."

Then, to Steve: "Nine zero degrees, Austin. Take her up on climb power."

Steve came around in his turn, rolled out to ninety degrees, feeding in power and trimming for the climb. Almost at once the gray mists enveloped the airplane. Steve studied the gauges and went to autopilot. He felt his body shaking as he sat back to monitor the instruments.

"Tom, give me a reading at twenty miles," he heard Franks say on the intercom.

"Eighteen miles now," the voice came back at once.

"Roger. Stand by," Franks said. He studied his watch, then spoke again into his mike. "We got twenty?"

"Twenty-three miles. Strong winds out there."

"Okay." Franks hesitated a moment. "Let her go, Tom."

"Confirm detonation signal," the voice said.

"Confirmed," Franks replied.

Instantly the dark gray sky pulsed, a sudden intense yellow glare that diffused everything around them. "What the hell!" Steve yelled, grabbing for the controls, scanning the gauges for the engine explosion and fire he suspected. Nothing. Everything was perfect. "I don't get it," Steve said. He looked through his window. The engines ran fine. He turned to the right. "Sam, the engines. You saw that flash—"

"There's nothing wrong with the engines."

"But that light. You *must* have seen it!"

"I saw it. But it was more than twenty miles behind us, Austin. Back at the *Dorina.*"

"The *Dorina?*"

"She's right in the middle of that weather. High winds, waves building. Even a baby nuke gets swallowed up without a trace."

He couldn't help the echo of his own words. Had he really been a part of this? "Baby nuke?"

"Right," Franks said, his lips stretched. "Only three kilotons. Leaving evidence around is stupid."

"But . . . but the ship!"

Franks looked at him.

"What ship?"

CHAPTER 14

It was all so incredible, yet every attempt to mask reality as fantasy was another dead end. There was some escape in the silence of thunder, the drone of the engines and roar of the wind. Something familiar to cling to as he tried to untangle his thoughts from a mixture of horror and rage.

They climbed to thirty thousand feet, where Steve leveled off the Nord, making final adjustments to the autopilot. Franks agreed to his request to take over control, and Steve slid back his seat to its fullest extension, leaning his neck against the headrest and closing his eyes. The gentle motion of the airplane swayed him into a deep stupor. He hoped for sleep, sought to drag it around him. It was no use.

He had gone in against targets in Vietnam with his savaging loads of cannon shells, rockets, bombs. He was a young pilot then, but had wanted none of it, wished his bombs would fall on empty trucks and was delighted and grateful when he got out with a few broken ribs, transferred to test piloting and got into the Apollo program.

On the other hand, he had once been a volunteer for the

élite FB-111 strike team, trained and presumably ready to knife deep into Russia with thirty megaton bombs. True perspective had waited for that first time he looked back across a quarter million miles of space to stare in wonder at the blue planet Earth, and uniquely sense the fragility of an entire world.

If that had never taken place, if he had remained in uniform, would he be so very different from what now repelled him in the person of Sam Franks? God, he hoped so. He had to believe so.

In a way, of course, he was still in uniform—trying to perform a mission. He wondered if he would be able to stomach it, and suddenly wished his employers—McKay and Goldman—were there to share the horror they'd assigned him to, however necessary and right their purposes. He twisted in his seat, taking in with a rush of gratitude the sweep of high altitude. Beneath them, at twenty-four thousand, a solid deck of clouds obscured the earth. The sun was behind them, sliding toward the clouded horizon, spraying the cottony world below with a scalloped pink. He had always found peace in this sight and now he especially needed its help.

He also needed the chance to get off somewhere with Marty Schiller and go over this madness. After this demonstration he realized in a new way that they didn't dare even mildly question Sam Franks and the organization—or discuss it where they might be overheard because of bugs in their rooms. He suddenly remembered Sam's words when he had pointed to the bedroom door in the apartment. "That's yours, Austin. You'll find a flight suit in your size in there. Your own boots have been repaired. Your personal things are on the dresser . . ."

Those boots were more fixed than repaired, he thought, doubtless with a pea-sized FM transmitter inserted into the heel of a flight boot, capable of picking up conversation within fifteen yards and transmitting it at least a hundred yards. The battery would last two weeks if left on twenty-four hours a day. Steve didn't need to dig into the heel of his boot. He already knew what he'd find there. He dragged up what he'd been taught by McKay and Goldman. The only thing you have the right to expect is the totally unexpected. Like filament radios. They're put together as flat as a sheet of paper and then they're literally woven into clothing, along with thin-wire antennas. The same with batteries; silicon wafer designs are about the most reliable. Buttons, zipper handles, the thicker lining in the crotch, armpits and neck bands.

Well, people like Sam Franks didn't survive because they were stupid, or neglected to protect themselves against enemies—real, potential and imagined. His own government did the same . . . The more he saw of Sam Franks, the more he realized the complexity and danger in his sense of righteous morality. Sam had his twisted convictions and he acted them out—never mind the consequences. Not for an instant did Steve doubt now that Sam Franks was directly involved with what had destroyed the Congo city of Butukama. Or that he could do something equally shocking again. In almost any city in the world. If the price was right, he *would* do it again.

Obviously, Sam Franks was only one cog in the wheel beneath which the Congo city had been annihilated. There were more people in the top hierarchy of his organization. They assigned the paramilitary operations to Sam. Others clearly were better equipped to work out payment, disburse funds, and do it all without revealing who and what they really were.

The Portuguese had been blamed for the destruction of Butukama—a red herring from the start? The Portuguese might have had their reasons, but somehow the evidence of Portuguese equipment and a body or two was a bit too convenient. More likely, Steve suspected, was a government uniquely paranoid about black power, black government, black control in Africa—the government of South Africa? Well, it might come out in the wash one day. And if it was South Africa, they'd so far kept their hands clean. All they risked was money. Whoever it was had *bought* Sam—Steve reminded himself that Franks no doubt had enough money to keep him in a lifetime of luxury. But was it only what had happened in SAC? Power? Satisfaction from manipulating people and governments, coloring history itself? A Dr. Strangelove complex? More than one man who possessed enormous power had gone through life convinced he was only a lonely actor on a stage, that life was simply a monstrous joke and death no more than ringing down a curtain.

His head was splitting when he felt a hand on his shoulder. "Want to take her down?" Franks asked.

Steve turned to the controls, closing off from his mind everything except the descent on instruments and the approach to the field located east of Oristano on Sardinia. He was able to lose himself for another hour on the ground. He made certain the airplane was parked properly and exacting service and maintenance started (another unbreakable rule Franks had brought with him from the Strategic Air Command). In the main, thick-walled command structure of Oristano they went through a meticulous medical checkup, where the doctors ordered atropine shots as a required safety procedure against any possible exposure to the nerve gas.

Finally, details out of the way, they went to the apartment now assigned permanently to Steve and Marty Schiller. Steve found the suite empty and was not surprised, since it would take some time for the special squads and other teams to be returned from the tanker. When Steve got back from his room in fresh clothes he found Sam Franks waiting for him.

"How does it feel, Austin? Fighter pilot to test pilot to astronaut, back to fighter pilot and now this. At least life hasn't been dull for you. Today you got to the other side of the fence, Austin. Two hundred people . . ."

Watch it, Steve warned himself. Sam was needling him, probably still testing him, seeing if he could push him into some self-serving defense that would betray his special status—if he had one. He had to be careful to play it very straight. Which, considering the disgust and anger he felt, wouldn't be hard.

"You make it sound as if *I* pushed the button. It was *your* order, not *mine*."

"So what? What's the difference? When they dumped those nukes on Hiroshima and Nagasaki, didn't the navigator have as much a hand in the deal as the pilot or the bombardier? He got them there. Same in this operation. And it's all the same package—don't try to separate things out by telling yourself the gas got 'em first. You don't *know* that everybody was laid out. You just don't know. Law is a funny thing, Austin. You can knock off one person—even if he's the kind that rapes kids—outside of their rules and you're a murderer. If you got a tin badge on your shirt you're a hero."

Steve shifted uneasily in his chair. Sam was almost exuberant, and Steve felt his earlier thoughts were very much on the right track. Sam Franks was a man convinced of the rightness of his way, the immorality of the rest of the world. A very dangerous man. A man never to be off guard with.

"I'll tell you something else, Austin. After what happened today you're as guilty by their rules as I am. Which still makes you, compared to the politicians who've been ordering up our wars, a saint." He held up his glass in a toast.

Jackson McKay came into his office in grim silence. Goldman knew the signs. Every move and expression of McKay's told him the session at the White House could have gone better.

McKay threw his coat across a chair, dropped heavily behind his desk. "The ship, no question but that it was nuclear."

"There was a storm there," Goldman said, "and the bomb wasn't that big, so—"

"I know, I know. Whoever destroyed that ship counted on the storm to wipe away the evidence. Normally it might have done so. But for a change we were in some luck. One of our nuclear submarines—part of the Polaris fleet that's on station—was about a hundred miles from the *Dorina* when the bomb exploded. They picked up pressure waves at that distance, and their search equipment got a fix on the general area. The Pentagon ordered them to the surface and to get their sensors out. Fortunately they were pretty much downwind of the blast. Even with a storm it's not easy to hide radioactive sodium. The stuff was still so hot some of the radiation counters went completely off scale."

"It still seems strange," Goldman said, "that anybody

would use a nuke to get rid of an ocean liner. Any chance it was political?"

"No," McKay said heavily. "CIA confirmed a quarter of a billion dollars worth of precious gems, jewelry. They haven't confirmed the customer. Just that it's somewhere in the Communist bloc. Anything on those computer runs on the pilots?"

They had been processing a meticulous trackdown of every top man in SAC who had left the organization and might not be accounted for. "We thought we had good leads on four men. Henry Williamson, Sam Franks, John Freeman and Bill Baxter. All former aircraft commanders. They're still in the flying business and they're all accounted for."

"Who determined that and how?" McKay demanded.

"We've run the checks, Jackson. Record of their whereabouts, who they fly for, where they live, confirmation through files and records and—"

"And so much thin air if someone *wants* to cover up their tracks," McKay broke in. "Doesn't anyone keep in his head that we're dealing with real professionals? Didn't they ever think, for example, of doubles? I suppose," he said acidly, "you've even got reports of our people observing these four?"

"Of course," Goldman said.

"It's not good enough, Oscar. Damn it, you get the word to our people that I want fingerprints. *Fingerprints* of each man. Just keep in mind how someone like Williamson or Franks or any of them might set up a cover by taking the time and trouble to locate a man who looks like himself, about the same age and build. The man's a pilot. If there's enough money involved and it's required, plastic surgery is always available. The man becomes a very serviceable double. A damn near spitting image made to order.

"All our man has to do then is play it the way he likes. Maybe he wants to knock out his own past. Maybe money is it. Whatever. But he is a man who wants to be in two very different places at the same time. The only way to check this, Oscar, the *only* way, is to get fingerprints and check them out with those we have on file, get them from

111

the FBI or SAC or whomever. And I want *you* personally to go over the prints we get. Do it *now*, Oscar. Get those prints taken as soon as possible."

Goldman got to his feet, prepared to leave. McKay stopped him. "Let me fill you in on the rest. The President's foremost concern is that these people are far beyond anything to do with money. I agree with that and I know you do too. That means they'll spend *anything* to protect their operation. They're actually a government unto themselves.

"The real question is, Oscar, what happens when these people decide to hold an entire city or even a small country ransom? It's likely to happen if they keep operating this way. They've already destroyed a city. And an ocean liner. When they decide to flex their muscles, God help us. It won't be any experiment. It will be a lesson in terror. And until we get more information, until we separate people from shadows and non-identities, there isn't any way we can stop them. And you know why?" McKay raced ahead in answer to his rhetorical question. "Because there are always people willing to sell out. They'll sell anything or anybody for the right price. Even if gutting a city with nukes is involved. The President, fortunately, is aware that if we ever manage to identify this group, we've got to move against them. We'll coordinate with the Russians, the British and maybe the French. It will be—"

"Self-preservation."

"But something else worries me."

"I know," Goldman said. "Steve. And Schiller."

"We won't be able to protect them. *If*, that is, they've managed to find out who they are. And *if* they've managed to get close to them. And they're still alive."

"I have the feeling they are," Goldman said.

"That won't hold up in an official report. Maybe it's wishful thinking, but I'm inclined to agree. Still, how do you explain gut feelings to the White House? Well, if Steve has somehow hooked on with this group, then he and Schiller may well have no way of communicating with us. If we do identify and locate the organization we'd have to move immediately. If Steve and Marty are there—"

"They get clobbered along with the rest," Goldman finished for him.

"Austin, you wonder why you already know so much about this outfit? What the hell could I tell you about Pentronics that anybody who wants to know can't find out? We're not only known throughout most of the world, we advertise in military and professional journals all through Europe and Africa. Pentronics actively solicits business."

Sam Franks reached for a fresh cigar. For more than an hour he had discussed the operations of the front organization. Despite what he had seen, Steve was still stunned to hear that Pentronics did more than three billion dollars gross annually, and this came from *open* contracts. He paid full attention to Franks, even as a part of him marveled that this same man talking easily and pleasantly with him could and had just as easily given the signal that wiped from existence every human being in an entire city.

"We're covered in every way," Franks continued. "We're the very model of a legitimate outfit. But if anyone ever does get on to us, he's got to be able to prove it. No, let me change that. He has to *survive* long enough to point the finger. We've a good record for taking care of people with long noses."

Steve remembered what he'd heard from Goldman and McKay. They'd lost a great many people—capable, experienced agents.

"Let's say we're caught red-handed," Franks offered. "Being caught is a long way from having someone *do* something about it. And who blows the whistle? And even if it's blown, who comes in to get us? It won't be any international organization, that's certain. They're too busy being paralyzed with bickering for us to worry about. So it would be an individual government, or at most a combination police and military action by one or two. Well, even that combination needs proof. We have contacts everywhere. We own a fairly choice assortment of officials and generals. But if it *all* goes to hell, there's the ultimate answer."

"Such as," Steve said, suspecting what the answer would be.

"Once your people are in someone else's hands, Austin, you can't keep them from talking. Between drugs and other techniques everyone talks sooner or later. So what happens even if an entire complex of ours is invaded or taken over? We erase it. We go in with an appropriate-sized nuke and we erase it *all*."

Franks studied the man sitting across from him. "You got pretty upset about today, didn't you?"

Steve nodded.

"Still shook?"

"I am."

"You ever get screwed up in the belly in Nam after one of your missions?"

"I threw up a couple of times," Steve said, his voice flat.

"Well, I'll tell you something. I know you and I know your background, and if you didn't feel the way you do right now, I wouldn't trust you. Changing what's been shoved into your skull all your life doesn't happen with a snap of the fingers. You've got to sweat it out of yourself."

"How about you, Sam. Did you go through it?"

Franks got to his feet with a sudden movement and began pacing the floor. He looked like an angry animal.

"I don't like being a sacrificial goat, Austin. If it's in the line of duty, that's different. *You* of all people know the score. You put your tail on the line and that's it. But you *don't* watch yourself get sold down the river, because that's a violation of everything you've been willing to *die* for."

He stopped suddenly. "One thing, Austin, bitter or not, whatever I did I made sure that *I* wasn't selling *my* country down the river. Nothing they'd done to me could make me do that. But I wouldn't just lay there on my back while some political animals walked all over me. *That* stopped right then and there. It hasn't and it won't change for me—"

He stopped as the apartment door opened. They both turned to see Mikhail Oleg standing in the doorway, looking at them with a strange air of hesitation.

"What the hell is the matter, Mike?"

114

Oleg glanced at Franks, turned to Steve. "Did you know the truth about him?" the Russian asked suddenly.

Steve felt his skin chill. "The truth about who?" he said, all the time knowing it must be Marty Schiller. He didn't miss the inflection in Oleg's voice, the use of the past tense.

"He is an agent—he was an agent for the CIA," Oleg said, the words clipped. "He was a fake, sent to infiltrate us. He conspired with his leaders," Oleg accused the absent man, "to dupe and use *you*, Austin, while trying to uncover us."

"Oleg, I don't know what the hell you're talking about," Steve said. He stood before his chair, his shoulders hunched.

"That is true enough," the Russian told him. "If it were not true, you would be dead this very moment." Oleg turned to Franks. "Schiller was acting. All the time. He led this fool"—he gestured at Steve—"into that fight in the television studio. Schiller made certain the Boeing would be where it was when they reached the airport. An escape!"

He walked slowly into the room, facing Steve. "The great Colonel Austin, manipulated every step of the way. They pulled the strings and he danced like a puppet. He—"

"Oleg, I'll break you in half."

"Hold it, Austin." The words snapped from Sam Franks. "Let him have his say."

"He's crazy, Sam. Marty could never—"

"There is no mistake," Oleg said. "We have the proof. Down to the fingerprints. When he was younger, Schiller was in the wartime OSS. How did we find out? The British government stupidly kept on file a secret record of Schiller. They never destroyed it. His fingerprints, everything. We managed to obtain that record. It is all there, every detail. It matched our suspicions and—"

"Then how the hell," Steve flared, "do you know *I'm* not a plant?"

Oleg laughed at him. "I said you were a fool, Colonel Austin, but you are not a spy. And Colonel Franks feels you have great potential. If there were the slightest evidence, suspicion, you would now be with your friend."

"Where is he, Oleg? I'll ask him myself. You can be there when I do. And if what you say is true, I'll—"

"You'll do nothing. There is nothing left to do."

"Where the hell is he?"

Oleg looked at Franks. "You did not tell him?"

"Tell me *what?*"

"That he was aboard the *Dorina* when the bomb went off."

CHAPTER 15

"Let's get the record straight," Sam said. "Schiller was your friend. I'm sorry you had to lose someone close to you. But like Mike said, Schiller *was* a plant. We checked it out coming and going, Austin, just like wo checked you out. Schiller was still active. This was his *assignment.*"

Steve knew if he was to continue his mission, there really wasn't anything more to say. He also knew that if he'd had the long background in this field that marked Schiller's records he'd also be so many free atoms floating in the sky.

Oleg had nailed it. The *British* secret files on Marty Schiller. What a rotten break. OSO had covered its records well enough. Sure, Marty had been in the wartime OSS. So what? Lots of people had done that sort of work. But the British were so proud of minute details, and some obscure office had kept up its file on Marty, and the records showed him moving from OSS to CIA and then to

OSO, and remaining active in his work. Giveaway. Oleg might not have been dead sure about his suspicions. There might have been some doubt. But from Oleg's viewpoint, and Sam Franks', so what? Marty wasn't *that* important. There were plenty of professional mercenaries around. So Marty, even if there was some question about him, was expendable. Oleg just had a sense of the macabre about him. Poetic justice and all that nonsense. No one could ever *prove* how Marty had been killed, because there weren't any witnesses. They were all dead.

But there was nothing about Steve Austin as an agent with OSO. Only that OSO had funded an experimental program involving multiple amputees. And Steve's appearance before those amputees was perfectly natural. He'd appeared at a dozen Veterans' Administration hospitals to demonstrate what could be done with bionics. A sort of personal Project Hope.

But no one by the name of Steve Austin existed in OSO records. A cover name had been assigned to him, and that cover name wasn't on paper. It was simply told to a very small group. So as far as all official records of OSO were concerned, even if they could be stolen, there wasn't a single mention anywhere of Steve Austin as a member of that group. As intended.

And the reason he was alive this very moment.

Later that evening Sam Franks told him they were going to disappear for a couple of weeks. Franks told him, "Knock off a city of blacks and you get wagging heads. Knock off a boat with all those gems and they're screaming for the terrible criminals. That's you and me, Austin."

"And so what do we do now?"

"What every successful criminal does. We are going on vacation, including a private villa at the Riviera—posh, sun and sand, private chef, and plenty of cooperative ladies."

In the weeks following, Steve Austin tried his best to will impatience from his mind, and to keep silent about the obscenity he felt in what he'd seen and been part of—and most personally the death of Marty Schiller. If he'd ever needed a special motive for seeing this thing

117

through, Marty's sacrifice had given it to him. Besides, there was no way out while they were on the Riviera, and there was so much more to this whole Pentronics operation and to Sam Franks he felt he still needed to know. OSO had programmed him. The instinct to bust out and blow the whistle now before another bomb went off could tip his hand too soon, allow the as yet unborn subsurface part of the organization to regroup, and risk an even more horrible catastrophe later. Breaking off the top of this malignant weed and leaving the roots might only spread and strengthen it.

Jackson McKay had even predicted this moment when he had told Steve he might even have to be involved in detonating a nuclear device. Well, there had been a nuke, if one of the smallest tactical ones, aboard the *Dorina,* and it had obliterated the ship and everyone aboard. Before he could break away from this crowd, *if* he could, he might be in a situation where another nuke would be brought to terrifying life. He had to weigh immediate horror to future horror on a wider scale. It was a position that would take time to adjust to—in the head and the gut. He needed those few weeks on the Riviera, and what Sam Franks had planned for a "shaking out" period afterward.

Sam lined it up in customary style. He pulled a Lockheed Jetstar from the Pentronics flight line and assigned it to their three-week fly-around-the-world. The Lockheed was a beautiful bird with four new bypass engines, an extra set of tanks slung beneath the wings. Sam provided false passports and a thick folder of identification papers for themselves, the airplane, and others with them. They had a relief team of two pilots and a navigator, and for "everything else," as Sam put it, a secretary, two stewardesses, and a versatile Girl Friday.

Sam had an unbreakable rule in that department. None of his people ever did *anything,* including drinking coffee, with a lady unknown to the organization. He'd once killed a man for violating that rule, which seemed wasteful until they drugged the woman and discovered her to be an agent for Interpol. They both had an accident driving on a mountain road in Italy—falling rock, a terrible accident, Sam explained.

118

The three weeks were especially useful to Steve, as Sam included in the tour an eyeball review of Pentronics facilities. By the time the trip was behind them, Steve felt he knew a great deal of value about the Pentronics organization and its facilities.

But there was no way to get the information back where it would do some good. Details of evidence were needed for the American government to move. Details alone would justify a secret meeting with the Soviet government. But he couldn't very well give an hour's worth of such information over a phone (*if* he could get a call through undetected), and if he couldn't leave the scene because of the interwoven security web of Pentronics what could he do?

Wait. Play his part. Do his job better than anyone else, because that's what Sam brought him in for, because anything less would qualify him for Sam Franks' dead-wood pile.

It was true there were apparent opportunities for Steve to steal a jet. With his bionics capabilities he knew he would have little problem killing a few guards and getting a bird off the ground. But most of the airplanes with any range to them never had fuel for more than a few minutes' flight. Basic security procedures.

There were others, however, that were kept fully fueled. Steve probably *could* have busted into one of those and taken off. He was no stranger to the maintenance hangars, following Sam's edict that "if you fly 'em, you also baby 'em."

Yet there was something *wrong* about the setup. Why keep most planes low on fuel at Oristano, except for the interceptors on hot alert, and allow others (faster than the interceptors) to be fully fueled? And within immediate reach?

Steve decided to find out. The Sabreliner they'd flown several times was up for a hundred-hour maintenance check. On the excuse that some handling problems about the airplane bothered him, Steve put on mechanic's overalls and spent a night working on the airplane with the maintenance crew. He got his own copy of the airplane manual and he went through the ship with the bird dog instincts of a man hunting his own survival.

In a way he found it. He'd spent thousands of hours in the past combing airplanes this way. And the Apollo spacecraft. Steve Austin wasn't just a pilot; he had his Master's in aeronautical and astronautical engineering. Combining expertise with experience, he'd eyeballed the guts of airplanes and spacecraft to the extent that he'd developed a sure instinct for the telltale trouble sign.

He found it in the tail. High up in the vertical fin. The Sabreliner had a late-model modification. The maintenance crew had installed an Emergency Locator Beacon inside the fin. Almost all aircraft flying international routes were required to have the ELB. In the event of a crash or a ditching the ELB, responding to shock of impact and deceleration or, activated manually, sent out a screeching radio signal that rescue aircraft could home on.

Steve saw the ELB, checked it out against the manual. Everything *looked* fine. He got down to exacting specifications, which was when he found it. The ELB he saw in the vertical fin was four inches longer than the model he studied in the airplane manual. He unhooked the wires to the ELB that permitted manual activation. Then he sat before the device with a bright floodlight and studied it. He found the thin antenna, disconnected it. A screwdriver opened the instrument. Steve didn't care about the ELB system. But that extra four inches.

Plastic explosives. Activated by radio signal.

Steal an airplane. Take off and away.

Sure.

And someone sends a radio signal and the whole tail blows off the airplane. Ships like the Sabreliner don't carry ejection seats or parachutes.

And there was something else.

He might get away: there were ways to cut the wires to any explosive charge. He could work on an airplane and cut the whole system out and leave that airplane in service. He could pick the right time and place. When the weather was right—rotten enough so he could lose himself in it—he could maybe bust out.

And then what? Pentronics would be on the alert. They

might still lose a base. Maybe several of them. As well as some of its people. It could be hurt.

But it wouldn't be put out of action, which was what counted. Steve knew they had to have some big bombs hidden. Doubtless only a few people knew where they were. And if he messed up what he was here to do and they lowered the boom on Pentronics, he might just be setting up some city for a revenge action. The idea of being responsible for the deaths of a million or more people didn't sit well with him.

So, time to end the fantasy and stick it out. Steve settled down to what he suspected could be a very long stay.

CHAPTER 16

"You'll meet them later today. At lunch. Sperry and Kuto." Sam Franks stood with Steve at the edge of a sheer cliff on the island of Capri, looking across the water to the harbor at Naples. It was a stunning day, fair-weather cumulus reaching the horizon in all directions. "They got in this morning," Sam continued. "I can tell you now that we've been heading for some time toward a major decision in this business. You can get the details later, but you should know you're involved." He turned to glance at Steve. "That's by invitation, Austin." There was a pause. "I think I'd like this to be the end of the line."

Sam had said the end of the line, which Steve could only assume referred to those actions of Pentronics that wheeled and dealed in international paramilitary activity. A fancy description for mass slaughter and destruction, he thought, with sudden anger. He wanted to fire a thousand

121

questions but knew better. You didn't push this man, and so far he'd brought Steve into his confidence at what he thought was the appropriate time.

Back at the villa owned by Pentronics, Steve listened. Little need to speak until these men asked for his opinion. Lunch went quickly, and Steve's appetite yielded to his fascination for the three men who'd created Pentronics and built into their organization a military force as powerful as that of many leading nations.

Jonathan Sperry, the financial and political mastermind.

Hiroshi Kuto, stocky, physically powerful, facially unreadable. A genius at logistics and industry and international trade, and at manipulating anything that came in big quantities.

And Sam Franks, military and organizational genius.

Steve didn't learn a thing, and long before the lunch was behind them he understood he'd been present to be studied and judged by Sperry and Kuto.

That night, in an underground room guarded by men personally selected by Sam Franks, in a room where no eavesdropping devices had ever been placed, the three leaders of Pentronics planned their final operation.

"We're agreed, then." Sperry looked at his two companions. "It's time for Pentronics to become what it appears to be to the world—a maintenance operation on Sardinia with NATO contracts as the main sources of revenue. We can let the international charter, cargo and other subsidiary units be dissolved or bought out."

Kuto nodded. "What else? I have ears everywhere. When governments who have fought each other for years begin to work together against us . . . only a fool does not retreat when his foes become so desperate they will risk anything—even cooperation. Do you know what will happen within a year from now? The Americans and the Russians, and perhaps the Chinese, will create a special force in the United Nations. It will be almost as good as ours, only out in the open." He indulged himself in one of his rare smiles. "It will have the backing of the great military powers in the world. We have fenced with them, but now they are ready to use the bludgeon."

Franks nodded. "To wrap it up we do one more operation. That ends it all."

"But *what* an operation," Sperry said. "It will be the strongest ransom note in history. One billion dollars in American currency."

"You said you had the essentials worked out, Sam," the Japanese said. "They are still the same?"

"The same. Atlanta, for reasons I'll detail later, remains the first choice."

Sperry leaned forward. "I thought you said getting one of the large bombs in there would be, how did you put it, Sam, too much exposure?"

"I've worked it out." He glanced from one to the other. "By the way, what do you think now of Austin?"

Sperry said, "He is the first man I have ever met who frightens me."

Franks glanced at Kuto. "I agree that he is unsettling."

"I'm going to use him on the weapon once in the city."

They stared at him. Franks waited them out. "Come on," he said impatiently as the silence dragged, "if you've got objections let's hear now."

"We know the rules," Sperry said. "Unless we can substantiate an objection we do not interfere with the others."

"No objections, then?"

"Only visceral," Sperry said.

"Why Austin?" Kuto asked.

"He's the best and most skilled weapons man around here, including myself. There's no way out of it. It's either him or me with the bomb, and I'll be too busy, as you know, with other matters."

Steve Austin was, for the moment, relaxing and, of course, unaware of the conversation between the three men.

He sat with his girl for the trip. Laura was a redheaded beauty, as charming as she was beautiful. They'd had dinner and now sat on the edge of a cliff overlooking the sea. She sat close to him.

He turned to her, touched her arm, and froze as she leaned forward, slumping. The warm sticky substance his fingers had detected was blood. He flattened against the rock, sliding closer to the cliff edge to gain advantage of the slight ledge he'd been seated on.

Another second, he would have been dead. There was no sound, but he saw no farther than an inch from his cheek a sudden pale flash as a bullet slammed off the rock. Instantly gravel clawed his face. He twisted, rolling to the side, placing the girl between himself and the top of the slope where the shots had been fired from. For a moment he felt embarrassed at using her body this way. Body. She was dead.

And she'd saved his life. The lifeless form twitched several times. Someone had a sniperscope on the slope's edge. The infrared scanner gave him a sight in the dark, and the silencer wiped away most sound. A dull *phhht* doesn't carry far in the strong winds blowing across the cliffs of Capri. Steve made certain he couldn't be seen by anyone looking downslope. He reached up to the girl's waist until he felt the warm blood from her body, got some on his hand and, keeping his arm low, smeared it across his face and neck. He maneuvered himself so that he lay sprawled on the rock, eyes staring vacantly, mouth open. It didn't take much to hold his breath. If only they couldn't hear his heart pounding.

He almost failed to hear the man who came to assure the death of his victims. A rubber sole slid across rock, Steve saw the dull gleam of moonlight from a pistol in a gloved hand. A silencer . . . they were here to guarantee the job.

He moved with his left arm—the bionics limb. His hand shot out. His powerful fingers smacked aside the gun and in a continuous movement closed around an ankle. Steve squeezed with strength enough to burst the skin and crush the bone beneath. He shoved, hurling the man to the side. He didn't wait to see what happened, figuring that where there was one there were usually two, rolling to his back again.

The second man dove at him with a knife. This was more in Steve's style. He stayed on his back, drew up his legs and kicked out. He felt something slice into his leg; the sensation told him something had slashed the plastiskin sensors, but the feeling was one of warning rather than pain. His steel-toed feet crashed into the man's chest, crushing the rib cage and lifting his victim into the air. Steve heard the body thump against the ground, followed by a rattle of stones and a truncated scream as the body fell away from the cliff. There wasn't time to think, he had to keep moving. He scrabbled along the ground, staying low, to reach his first victim, who had an ankle with white bone protruding in splinters. Steve took hold of the man and lifted him as high as he could.

Almost at once the body jerked as bullets smashed into the neck and head. Blood sprayed and the man went limp. Steve shoved him aside and picked up the pistol. The range was probably too great, but it was worth a try. He risked a quick glance over the ledge—there, barely visible against the skyline. Head down again, he moved to the side, popped up and emptied the gun. The hissing of the shots mixed with tiny splashes of flame. But whoever was looking through that sniperscope would at least know that someone was shooting back. Steve gambled he would run.

He threw aside the gun, took a deep breath, and started up the cliffside in a twisting run, his bionics legs pumping. By the time he reached the top, along the walk, no one was in sight.

Sam Franks studied the shell casing under the light. "Thirty-thirty," he said finally. "Hunting rifle, high velocity." He tossed the shell to Mikhail Oleg, who held it in his hand. "You say you never heard any shots?" Franks asked Steve.

"No shots," Steve told him again. "He had a silencer on the rifle, and the one who came down the hill had a silencer on the hand gun. You got the weapon yet?"

"They're looking for it now. I hope it didn't go over the cliff. It might give us a lead. I don't like this. Not just that someone took a couple of shots at you, Austin. Bad enough. The fact that there were at least *three* of them. That I especially don't like."

"I'm getting the idea that someone doesn't like me," Steve said.

"Someone goes after you, it means he doesn't like *us*. I

was tied up with John and Hiroshi. Mike, here, was inside the villa with some other people. You happened to be the perfect available target. It could have been any of us. The girl is dead, and it's bad luck you killed both those guys." He shook his head. "If one of them had lived we would have made him tell us his life story." Franks looked at Oleg, then back to Steve.

"Got any suggestions? Especially since you were the target?"

"Tighten security?"

"We're so tight right now a flea couldn't scratch his rear without our knowing it. This job is from the inside. Someone has managed to get to some of our people."

"Any ideas?"

"I'll be working on it. Meanwhile, none of us is ever alone. And if I were you, moon man, I'd sleep with my one good eye wide open."

They didn't try again for nearly ten days and then it was in Sevilla, Spain. Steve had yet to be told the details of what he already knew was the culmination of Franks' operations with Pentronics, but he could dream up some ugly notions by Franks' order to "get sharp again" studying the systems manual for a 32-megaton hydrogen bomb.

They were in Sevilla for a meeting with Kuto's logistic people. Normally Steve might not have come along, but after the episode on Capri Sam kept his top team together wherever possible. To sustain security in the hotel, Pentronics rented three complete floors. The Pentronics team stayed in the center floor, in the core of the building. Security people occupied the floor above and the one below, as well as the rooms surrounding the center. Elevators weren't allowed to open on the three floors unless at least two of Franks' men were on the scene. Because they would be locked up at the hotel for several days, Franks had also brought along several accommodating ladies, all well known to them and considered beyond suspicion. Franks believed the theoretical security risk was offset by their contribution to easing off the pressure of this highly charged session.

Steve wanted none of it. He still remembered Laura's

126

blood on him from the shootout on Capri. More than that, more than anything else, was the association once again with the terrifying hydrogen bombs. A 32-megaton bomb doesn't damage a city. It doesn't spread death and destruction. It's a thousand times worse. You think of the bomb and that star raging in its center and that's bad enough, and then you think about when it's over, except that it isn't because one of these things rigged with an outer shell of thorium or dirty U-238 means intense, terrible fallout that persists for longer than anyone wants to know.

Understanding the nature of the beast was Steve's especial curse. He knew by his study assignment that he'd doubtless somehow be locked in with the weapon. And there wasn't the slightest consideration on his part of getting out now even if he could, because Sam and his people might already have emplaced the weapon, and he'd picked up hints that this time they were going right into the front yard of the United States. Steve had to go along with it, hope for a chance to frustrate the plan, escape and get to where he could blow the whistle on the entire operation. Most of all, to do something about the bomb when and if that time came. Besides, the closer he was to the States the better. It all added up to his being as sharp as possible concerning the thermonuclear weapon. The more he knew about it the better his chances for pulling the plug when the critical moment came. If only he knew where and when . . . He went to sleep silently cursing the many corridors of possibility. No choice, really, but to push them aside and take things as they came.

Sometime in the middle of the night he heard his door coming open—a string taped on the door to the wall so that when the string moved, as the door opened, it knocked over a glass. Instantly he was awake, a .38 snub-nosed special in his hand and the hammer back.

In the dim light of the open door he saw a naked woman. Long blond hair, moving slowly to the bed.

"What the hell do you want?"

"I was told you were expecting me," she said, moving to his side. He felt stupid with the gun in his hand as cool, practiced fingers moved along him.

"Someone told you wrong." Perfume came from her in

127

what was almost a cloud "Now kindly get the hell out of here."

"What's wrong? Don't you want—"

The warning signals were in his head. He shifted position as she started to her feet; then she turned, looking down at him. Her hands fluffed the pillow. "I could please you," she said.

"I've never shot a woman but there's always a first—"

She caught him completely by surprise. The pillow ended up across his face. For a moment it blinded him, threw his balance off as he moved to throw it aside. He had only a glimpse of a knife slicing down at his chest. Instinctively he moved his right arm to ward it off. He'd forgotten about the gun as steel slashed his forearm. Burning stabbed him as he spun away from his attacker, rolling off the bed. He tried to bring his right arm up with the gun but he knew he was moving slowly. He saw the blade coming down again and he swung wildly with his left arm. A cry of pain followed the blow, and the woman was gone from sight.

Steve struggled to his knees, dizzy, trying to focus his eye. He heard a door slam. The gun was still in his hand. He lifted his right arm with his left, squeezed off three shots that sent hammering explosions through the room and, he knew, to the other rooms and the corridor outside. If nothing else it would bring the guards. He slumped back against the side of the bed, feeling damn foolish.

The doctor, who was always with them on major trips, told him he was lucky, that he had a deep wound but it was clean and would heal quickly, only six stitches. "Had it gone deeper or even just to the side . . ." He finished the stitches, secured the arm in bandages and finished off with a tetanus shot and massive dose of antibiotics.

Sam Franks waited with Mikhail Oleg until the doctor was gone. Steve told them what had happened in complete detail.

"First," Sam said, "no one set up any female visitor for you tonight. But whoever sent her in here knew it was the only way someone you didn't know could get inside your door." He shook his head in mild disgust. "You damned heroes . . . why the hell didn't you at least shoot her in the leg? We at least would have had a hand on them that way."

Steve didn't answer. Oleg asked him, "Did you recognize her, Austin?"

"No. I told you what I saw was in pretty dim light. She was tall. Sort of thick in the waist, long blond hair, like I said. Now that I think back on it, one thing surprises me. I've seen enough of your women, Sam, to expect a certain type. This one was about as flat-chested as they come."

"I agree," Franks said. "She's not from our group. Anything else?"

"I know I got a good whack at her. Don't know where I hit her, but wherever it was she'll carry a considerable bruise in a day or two."

Franks nodded. "That's it?"

"That's it."

But it wasn't, though Steve didn't realize it until early the next morning.

There was something about Oleg . . . he tried for hours to put his finger on it but kept missing it. Then it came back. The woman's perfume. Unmistakable.

The scent had gotten stronger for a while. During the time when Franks and Oleg were in the room.

Oleg. The damned perfume was on him too.

Which meant he had to know who the woman was.

CHAPTER 17

Several weeks before the first attempt on his life, Steve Austin was the principal topic for discussion at an estate outside of Bordeaux. None of the tightly knit group headed by Sam Franks was aware of this discussion and the conclusion reached except for Mikhail Oleg.

He had flown to the French city of Bordeaux with Jonathan Sperry and four of their best security men. Oleg went along as pilot of the Sabreliner and had no part in a conference for which Sperry was having to work out financial details with a member of the French government regarding a Pentronics supply operation that would also take them to the United States.

A woman, well known to the Pentronics group, having worked with them in the past, was admitted to the hotel room where the guards were told Oleg waited for her. She was met by two security guards, her papers examined. Oleg vouched for her in advance.

Yvette Rochelle remained in the room for approximately thirty-five minutes. When she left, she carried a note from Oleg which she showed to the guards. "I will return in two hours, perhaps a little more," she told them. "If you wish you may confirm this with Monsieur Oleg."

The guards smiled, asked no further questions of Oleg. To do so they would have risked their necks.

The woman left the hotel and went directly to the parking lot, driving off to the east. Eighteen miles from the hotel she turned from the main road and traveled another mile along a narrow country road to an isolated estate.

Here she was stopped at a heavy iron gate. She was questioned by guards, who directed a television transmitter at the vehicle. The guards were told to let her through at once.

Inside the estate, Yvette Rochelle removed her coat and conversed intensely with three men for an hour. The men were all high members of the Soviet secret police.

"Time is short," she told them. "I am more than ever convinced that Austin is working actively for his government, and that his escape from the United States was a well-planned charade. We were fortunate through our British contacts to find evidence of Schiller's agent status with the CIA for some years. Our Washington people could find nothing on him in CIA files there, but apparently the British are either sloppier about destroying incriminating records, or perhaps they—especially the late Mr. Schiller—are victims of the archivist's mania for keeping records, no matter what. Austin had been very effective, playing the role of Schiller's dupe, which Franks wants to accept because he needs Austin. I suspect he even likes him. I also suspect he works for OSO, although they have managed to obliterate all evidence of his association with them."

The leader of the Russian group played a mild devil's advocate. "You say that he has been involved in operations. That means he has been responsible for the deaths of many people. A cold-blooded effort. He does not seem to have the background for this. It is out of character with the man."

"You do not understand," Yvette Rochelle said angrily. "It was a situation where he did not play a direct part in causing the death of anyone else. Besides, you are rationalizing about the mind of another man. It is easy to do that, but not reliable. If he did not push a button or pull a trigger, he could do his own rationalizing. And what do we know about him? He is a combat veteran; do not forget that. He has been an astronaut. More than this, he is the wreck of a man. No legs, one arm, one eye. I will tell you he shows only token reluctance about killing when it has proved necessary. And the more I watch him, the more I see his carefully developed friendship with Franks, the

131

more convinced I become that he is an agent for the Americans."

"But if we are wrong—"

"If! Time is running out. You three are aware of the reports from Moscow. The Americans, like ourselves, are being embarrassed by this Pentronics group. The United States is actively trying to find out all they can about Pentronics. They need details, evidence, and Austin is in the perfect position to supply this information. We know what we have managed. Why not the Americans as well? It makes sense for both of us. Sam Franks is a former pilot for their strategic air force. Do they know Franks directs their military operations? If Austin has reported on Franks, then they know. If he has not yet done so, he will very soon.

"Once the Americans suspect Franks they can easily kill him. But is that their wisest course? If they kill Franks, another man steps in to take his place. Pentronics is an octopus. It reaches everywhere. Who knows where they have placed their bombs?"

The leader of the Russian group became impatient. "Get to the point," he told her.

"Pentronics is ideal for paramilitary operations controlled by the Americans," she said. "Steve Austin, I am convinced, is their hope for bringing Franks and the entire organization under their control."

Somewhat to her surprise, in view of the previous show of skepticism, she found agreement.

"We have been moving toward this same conclusion," she was told. "This concept is in favor in Moscow. We believe there is growing evidence the Americans are trying to make a deal with Pentronics. To buy them off—not with money, of course, but with protection for Franks and his criminals to do the dirty work of the Americans. They would function as a disassociated apparatus of the CIA and other groups. It's typical of the Americans, they stop at nothing and—"

"And neither will you," the woman broke in. "I am running short of time and you would please me to save your speech for another occasion. We are attempting to do the very same thing that Austin is here to do." She smiled. "We are not that much different."

The man looked at her. "We seem not to share Austin's success."

"That would be different if I had more support! And if Moscow would do what I have—"

"Enough. Time, as you say, is short. The question is what do we do about Austin?"

"He must be killed," the woman said immediately. "If we, if I, have been wrong . . . a dead American is of no concern to us, especially a man who, so far as the world knows, ran out on his country. Now, time is shorter than any of you know. They are planning something very big. It involves their going to the United States. If I am right, that will be the time and place for Austin to do everything possible to recruit Franks."

She studied the men with her. "Who knows what second thoughts Franks has had about what he is doing? Austin may persuade him he can regain favor with his government. And never forget that Franks has a genuine admiration for this man."

The leader of the three men said, "Can Austin buy him off?"

"No, no," the woman said impatiently. "What good is money to a man who already has millions? Austin can only offer what appeals to Franks. And that includes, I am convinced, full amnesty from his government and the freedom to continue doing just what he does now—except that instead of being an international criminal he will be a restored patriot in the secret employ of his government. Once again, I remind you that they will be in the United States soon. That is when Austin must make his move, and it is why we must stop him before that time arrives."

The answer came at once. "All right, then. But make it seem the Americans are responsible. We will make this plausible by convincing Franks that Austin *was* an American plant, that they were worried that Austin was betraying or soon would betray his cover by becoming overly friendly with Franks. Rather than risk this possibility, they murdered him. If, as you say, Franks might be receptive to

133

a proposal, Austin's death by American hands will alienate him all the more from the U.S., and most importantly, direct his interest toward working for us."

The woman left immediately for her car. She returned to the hotel and was cleared by security to go up to Oleg's room. Again she remained for about an hour. The telephone rang in the guards' room.

"Oleg here. The woman Rochelle will be leaving now. She will not return. Pass her through."

"Yes, sir. Good night."

Yvette Rochelle disappeared.

The first attempt to kill Austin came on Capri.

The second was made in Sevilla.

All Steve Austin knew was that whoever wanted him dead was almost certain to try again.

CHAPTER 18

Grand Slam was the code name Sam Franks assigned to his final operation. With round-the-clock protection assured him, Franks turned to the immediate needs of the Grand Slam operation. He brought a Douglas DC-6B four-engine transport to Oristano and had the old combination airliner-and-cargo ship tuned to perfection. Sperry arranged for cargo flights from Europe to Africa, on to Brazil and then northward into the United States. Within three weeks of starting the camouflage for Grand Slam, Pentronics was running ten transports of different types on the Europe-Africa-Brazil-United States route. On paper the operation was ordinary and beyond suspicion. The airplanes were searched regularly by Customs in the States, and regularly they were passed through, soon becoming familiar sights to government and airport officials.

Everything was going as planned. Steve Austin and Sam Franks virtually lived in their DC-6B. They flew almost constantly, returning to Europe from the States by the North Atlantic. When they were too tired to fly, a relief crew took over. Franks made certain that whenever the airplane was entering or leaving the United States, it was himself, and Austin, whose names were on the crew lists, manifests, customs and other forms. Not the name "Steve Austin," of course. On all paperwork he was listed as "Mike Arnold."

At first Steve wondered about flying into the States. After all, his face was hardly unknown. The last man on the moon, the desert crash, and above all that free-for-all in the television studio. He needn't have worried.

Sam Franks had arranged so that anyone who saw Steve Austin saw someone else. A makeup expert had done a job on him. A dark wig. A home-grown moustache. His normal light color gone under heavy dye to form a thick, black bush. Pilot's sunglasses. He always wore a heavy, bulky jacket that seemed to add thirty pounds to his body. Result—exit Steve Austin, enter "Mike Arnold."

Their cargo loads were authentic. The manifests listed special printing presses and associated equipment. When Customs decided to get into the guts of the presses one flight, Franks protested. Steve knew a charade when he saw it. Sam never wasted his breath on petty grievances or complaints. He watched with Sam as the crates were opened and gleaming new presses showed beneath. All but one crate.

The Customs chief tapped the wood. "What's in this one, Captain?" he asked Franks.

Franks sighed. "Ain't you seen enough, for God's sake?" He chewed the stub of a cigar and looked exactly as he wanted—a man who'd just flown a long and wearisome trip who wanted to get the hell to a bed.

"The case," insisted Customs. "What's in it?"

"Special ink, man. Just ink."

Pinchbars and screwdrivers opened the case to reveal a suspicious drum within. Customs didn't accept the contin-

135

ued explanations of special ink. They tapped a collapsible metal plug. Fifty-five gallons of ink that stained everything it touched gushed along the floor of the airplane.

The howls from Sam Franks could be heard for a mile.

Sam also made sure not to clean the airplane. The ink had run out the cargo door and left a huge ugly streak along the side and belly of the DC-6B. Sam left it there.

You could spot that particular DC-6B a mile off, which seemed exactly what Sam had in mind. Four times they flew into the States and four times they went through Customs and continued on to Atlanta. They stayed with the airplane as the cargo was off-loaded. Then, in a group that included four tough, no-nonsense security people, they took rooms at an airport motel. Early the next morning they were gone. It was a spartan existence that sharply contrasted with the luxury they'd known in the past.

On each of these flights Steve felt he had opportunities to break free. He could have made a good try at killing Sam to prevent what he intended to do—whatever that was. He could have crash-landed the airplane in such a way as to get the attention of the authorities. But what would he have told them? If Sam Franks died, Grand Slam would hardly suddenly be revealed or necessarily die with him. Sperry, Kuto, Oleg and the others would be likely to modify the plan and press to its conclusion. And there was always the possibility that Sam was running him, Steve, through some final diversionary test of his loyalty.

Reluctantly, Steve accepted the need to continue playing his role. He needed to wait until the moment he had the information that could not only stop Grand Slam but also assure the end of Pentronics and its secret alliances.

They were on their fifth flight to Atlanta when Sam said to him, "The key to this operation, at least where this old clunker is concerned, is for people to accept the sight of the bird. Not just *seeing* it, Austin, but accepting it as a part of the background and sliding into a slot in their thinking. We're going to be so common to these people that our *not* showing up when expected would bring out the hounds."

They had Atlanta in sight. Steve was flying this trip, rolling in steadily toward the airport under radar vectors.

"We're going to offer Uncle Sam a deal, and we're going to keep our end of the bargain," Sam went on.

Steve rolled out onto a long final approach to the runway, dropping gear and flaps and setting up the transport for its final descent. When Steve had her in the slot, Franks said:

"So the kicker in this whole thing is to put on the squeeze, put it on so hard that the other guy's eyeballs start to bulge. You can take off the pressure by bargaining so long as you leave no doubt you'll keep your side of the bargain. Then you can deal." Steve glanced from airspeed and altitude to the expanding runway. He watched the numbers slip beneath the nose of the DC-6B as he added a touch of trim to start the flare. "What happens, Sam, if the other side decides not to play by your rules? Like they say, it only takes one guy out of two to start a hassle."

Rubber squealed on macadam and the nose gear sighed gently to the runway. Steve let her roll without reversing the props; they wanted the far end of the runway for their turnoff.

"Yeah, but bargains work two ways. They don't keep their side, why, that's when it pays off to have had a very big stick in your hands all the time. That's when we go for broke and to hell with the consequences. You got to live by the threat you make.

"So if they sit down to deal with us," Sam said with a barely perceptible change of tone in his voice, "and decide to stick it to us, why, they are merely going to lose a city and an awful lot of its citizens."

So it was coming out finally. It had to be Atlanta or somewhere near. Steve kept a straight face, concentrating on taxiing the big airplane, trying not to reveal the shock effect of Sam Franks' words, realizing that the man had lived with this thing for so long it had become almost commonplace to him. He had no sense of its horrifying effect on Steve. Okay, Steve thought, at least keep talking, Sam . . .

"Of course," Sam said, "numbers don't really mean a damn anymore. It's not the numbers. It's *how* you lose the crowd. I mean, if you get a bad press out of it, something like that. A million Asians get knocked off by a storm or a famine and it rates a couple of inches on page forty. A hundred people die in an airplane crash in the middle of a city and everybody gets gas pains over it. At least we pick time and place, dealer's choice, and we're stacking the deck."

He turned to look at Steve. "You know how much we're going for, Austin? A billion dollars. A million clams a thousand times over. Sounds like a lot, doesn't it? It's really cheap. You figure the physical damage we can do, the panic we can let loose in every city in the country, and getting off the hook for a billion is bargain day. But we've got to make this deal stick, and that's where you and I come in. Sperry and Kuto will take care of the financial end. They'll move the money into shipping and industry and land. They know how to make it disappear so that it never surfaces."

Steve maneuvered the airplane into its assigned position on the cargo ramp. He went through the shutdown check list and they both watched the big props grind to a halt. Steve leaned back in his seat and released his straps. "Sam, we going to make a lifetime habit of this?" He gestured to the instrument panel and the cargo loaders rolling to the transport. "Whatever you've got in mind there's got to be a more interesting way to get there."

Franks laughed and slapped him on the shoulder.

"Soon, moon man. Very soon."

It was their next flight in the DC-6B. Coming out of Brazil Sam filed his flight plan to clear Customs in West Palm Beach rather than in Atlanta. Steve fidgeted at the unexpected change but gave it no more than that. It just didn't have that much significance.

He was wrong. They were still cruising at 22,000 feet when Sam began pulling the string.

"Double-team security is the kind of system that works a couple of ways," Sam began suddenly. "We're moving the bomb into Atlanta today."

Just like that.

"We've got security people all over the place."

So that's why the extra people on this thing with us . . .

138

"We got more than that nuke in Atlanta. We got a couple of other surprises for the people. You, moon man, are one of our specials."

Don't quit now, Sam. Keep talking, for God's sake . . .

"We also have a ship in the harbor at San Francisco. You know, it takes in Frisco and Oakland Bay. There's more than a hundred big ships in there at this moment and one of them is carrying a ten megatonner. *That* is our insurance."

Sam broke off suddenly, studying the navigation instruments. "How far out from West Palm?"

Steve watched the DME needle. "Little less than two hundred."

Sam nodded. "Start your letdown in five, Austin. We'll do it by the numbers."

"Right."

"Ever since three days ago nobody in this thing has blinked his eyes without being watched by two men assigned to him. That includes you. And me. And everyone else. Your two friends, Austin, are behind us in the bird right now."

"Interesting."

Sam laughed. "You're going to get real chummy with them, moon man. You see, we're going to leave the four of you together in Atlanta."

The four of us? What the devil can he—

"You, your two shadows, and the bomb."

My God . . .

"And we're arranging for you and the guards, right along with that big ugly thing, to be captured."

Steve glanced at Sam, who was watching him. "You don't look so good. I don't know whether you're confused or just plain shook."

"Try some of both."

"I'll fill in the rest." He paused to watch Steve roll in nosedown trim. The DC-6B began a long, flat descent. Their flight plan called for them to take her on down to fifteen hundred feet twenty miles due east of West Palm Beach before turning west and penetrating the ADIZ. It was all normal enough. They'd be in radar and radio con-

139

tact all the way through the Air Defense Identification Zone. "Keep her twenty miles off the coast," Sam reminded him.

"Twenty it is," Steve answered. He wondered why Sam was so insistent on details today. He brushed aside the question for another that hammered through his brain. The bomb was going into Atlanta *today*. But *how*, and where was it right now? It couldn't be aboard the DC-6B because they were going through Customs and those people hadn't let off an inch in their scrutiny of the cargo.

"So we set it up for the government to get their hands on you, your two shadows, and the bomb," Sam said. "Now, there are rules to every game, and the rules for this one are that none of you, *or the nuke*, can be touched. How's *that* for frustration!"

Steve busied himself for a moment with the throttle quadrant before he spoke. "All right, Sam, let's consider it next week and time for another thrilling episode. What happens after they get hold of us?"

"Once we have three-way confirmation through Sperry that the government has paid off the billion, *that's* when we let them know where *you* are."

"You're losing me, Sam."

"Sorry, I got ahead of myself. We set you and the bomb in Atlanta, right? Now, how do they know the bomb is the real article? Simple. It used to be one of theirs. When we contact them we give them its serial numbers. No questions, they know the bomb is missing. Hell, they've been *looking* for it, and now it turns up in their back yard.

"And what about the moon man? How do they know he's authentic? First, they receive a set of your fingerprints. They get photographs of you—and we've taken plenty of them these last few weeks—and they get a good look at that clean-cut, All-American face of yours. But how do we prove you've been right here in Atlanta? We tell them to get the tower voice tapes, you know, the automatic recordings they keep for a month at every control tower in the country. We tell them what times we've flown in here. You've talked to approach control and the tower. So we tell them to get the tapes and play them back, and then, to get the tapes of your voice when you were flying as a test pilot and an astronaut. They do a voice ID. They check one against the other. What do they find? That 'Mike Arnold' is really their moon man who took off against God and country. Steve Austin himself. There's no question, none at all."

Steve paused to jockey the controls. Sam glanced at him, cigar clenched in his teeth.

"Well, that's how it goes," Sam said. "All leaves no doubt in their pointed heads that we've got the goods and we've got you. There are some other details, Austin, but they don't concern you. They'll work, don't you sweat it. You just sit tight with that big pineapple while we negotiate. Think of it as a vacation. You don't have to do a damned thing except play nursemaid."

So my real job, Steve thought, is establishing credibility for the basis of their monstrous blackmail operation. And if it goes wrong, well, I'm just another casualty. Good old Sam . . . a real romantic—with somebody else's life . . .

"They pay off," Sam went on, lighting a fresh cigar, "and they get a roadmap telling them where to find you. They find you, they know we've leveled with them so far. They also find the bomb. You're in their hands, but not really. They disarm the nuke. And that, friend, when they're all relaxed and putting on clean shorts, is when you tell them about the device aboard that ship in Frisco harbor. What do they do now? They send you and the boys on your way, safe and sound, right? When you're safe and have been swallowed up somewhere in the world, they find out where the bomb is in Frisco."

"It's quite a scenario. I wonder if they'll buy it."

"They'll make it a best seller. Listen, you're forgetting who *you* are, what you stand for. But if that isn't enough they'll have thirty-two million tons of hell in the living room with them. They've *got* to believe *that*. And that kind of belief is our double insurance. Because if they decide to play games . . . Frisco and Oakland *disappear*. And they won't know how much more they might lose. That's where keeping our word comes in. We've got to play it straight, and we *will*."

He shifted in his seat and slid closer to the controls. He held his hands over the yoke and turned to Steve. "Time for me to earn my pay. I'll take it down."

At fifteen hundred feet he rolled the DC-6B to the left and came out on a heading that would bring them precisely seventeen miles north of the airport at West Palm Beach. Steve noted the darkening sky. Until now their time of arrival had meant little to him. Suddenly it seemed important, a part of the awful fabric Sam Franks was weaving. They pounded through light turbulence at their same altitude, Sam talking to the air traffic controller at West Palm, knifing through the ADIZ exactly on schedule, and being called off from the ground. Sam switched radio frequency to radar approach at West Palm and got his acceptance to continue to the field. They passed over the shoreline and Sam began the wide pattern to the south. He kept looking to his right and Steve followed his gaze.

"You see it?" Steve asked. Another plane, coming in toward them.

"I got 'em," Sam said. He surprised Steve by reaching to the control panel and switching their lights on and off five times. Steve kept the other plane in sight and saw bright landing lights flash on exactly five times.

"Right on time," Sam said.

They were well to the west of the airport now, and down to less than a thousand feet. Sam kept going down and leveled off finally at four hundred. Steve started to comment on their low height but thought better of interfering.

The other airplane kept closing in on them. Steve couldn't believe it. *The other ship was an exact duplicate of their own DC-6B, right down to the serial numbers and the huge stain along the side and belly of the fuselage.*

He knew then what was happening. It was quite a move. The other airplane slid into tight formation. Anybody following them on radar (and they were almost too low for that) would get only a single blip painted on a scope from the transponder of the second airplane. Exactly as intended.

Steve slipped his headset over his ears. He knew what

142

would happen next and he wasn't disappointed. The pilot in the second airplane, using the same numbers as their own ship, using the same company name, called in to the tower for landing instructions.

"Three Six Six Delta, maintain wide left base. Report turning final."

Even as the words came in from the tower operator, Sam knuckled the yoke forward. The DC-6B dropped to a breathless two hundred feet and roared away to the west in a tight turn. The second airplane eased back to eight hundred feet, coming in clearly now on the radar scope at West Palm. As that ship went on to land at West Palm—ostensibly on the flight from Brazil—Sam flatted his plane to the west over open swampland.

Two hundred feet. Then a hundred, and still he eased the big airplane down. The altimeter was useless. Palmetto and scrub brush whipped crazily toward them, racing by. *They were off the radar screen. No way for radar to follow them. Not this low.* Sam had to keep this up for only a few more minutes and then he could start a gradual climb. No one would ever know about the connection between the two airplanes. No one would ever suspect there were two planes with identical appearance. It was neat. Customs would check out an airplane they believed had come in from Brazil. Everything would be in order.

And meanwhile Sam Franks would be delivering a hydrogen bomb to Atlanta.

They landed in Atlanta on a flight plan filed with Ormond Beach, Florida, just north of Daytona Beach, as the point of departure. No tower at Ormond Beach, no need to be suspicious. They taxied to the familiar cargo area, but there all familiarity with past operations ended. Several trucks rolled up to the plane, effectively screening it from any intruders. Steve was certain that every man there was heavily armed. He waited in the cockpit while Sam personally supervised unloading a heavy crate onto a truck. He called to Steve to join him in the vehicle, and almost at once they rolled from the airport, the middle truck in a convoy of three.

It was dark as they pulled up before a three-story apartment house somewhere in Atlanta. The truck went into a garage and a team of men were at work immediately opening the crate. Steve and Sam watched as a heavy metal container was rolled to the center of the living room on the first floor.

"We took over this building four months ago," Sam explained. "No one pays any attention to the trucks. They've been coming and going around here all that time. Now, watch."

Nothing left to chance. The metal container weighed, Steve estimated, somewhere between 180 and 200 pounds. A section of the ceiling was removed, and a winch sling and hook placed about the container. An electric motor raised the container to the second floor, where it was rolled into a bedroom. The ceiling—the floor for the second-floor apartment—was put back in place and the winch removed to the truck in the garage. Moments later the truck rolled away.

That left six men in the apartment. Steve, Sam Franks and two guards—now openly displaying submachine guns —for each of them. Two guards stayed in the bedroom and the other two took up position elsewhere.

Sam opened a heavy toolbox and laid out on the floor an array of special tools and instruments. He connected testing devices to the container, triple-checking every move he made, and calling on Steve to provide a fourth check.

"Got it?" Sam finally said to Steve.

Steve nodded. His throat was dry, his voice rasping. "Got it. The device is checked out. It can receive its detonate signal on two primary channels. You've removed four of the six safety interlocks."

"Anything else?"

Steve swallowed. "Only one of the two remaining interlocks is part of the auto system. The other is manual."

"Which I will release," Sam told him, "before I leave. I'll trip it and that leaves one. Which is, well—*you* know."

An hour later it was done. Steve had his instructions. The apartment was well stocked with food, medical supplies and whatever was necessary for a week's stay.

"There's a telephone here," Sam explained. "This way we can always reach you if we need to. But don't—and I repeat *do not*—make any calls out of here on that thing. It'll blow up in your face, Austin. The two guards stay here with you. One watches you at all times while the other breaks."

Steve looked at them. Sloppy, in greasy clothes, stubble on their faces, beer cans lying around. Each beer can was capable of an explosive release of Mace.

"No one leaves this building," Sam said, "until you get word to do so."

"Which is when?"

Sam handed him an envelope. "Your instructions are in there. You open this thing four hours after I leave. Everything you need to know is in there, Austin. And that envelope is like the phone. *Don't* open it in less than four hours. It's got a timed-decay acid inside and it'll blow up in your face if you touch it before it breaks down and becomes harmless."

He handed Steve the envelope, clasped his hand and looked at Austin for a long moment. Then, strangely, he nodded and left, followed by his two watchdogs. A door below closed and Steve heard a heavy metal bolt slam.

Steve looked about him. He was in an isolated building on the second floor with an explosives-rigged envelope of instructions, a telephone waiting to blow up in his face, and two well-trained killers.

And a hydrogen bomb capable of destroying the city of Atlanta and all its suburbs.

With only a single safety interlock to prevent just that from happening.

CHAPTER 19

He looked at his watch.

Four hours and eight minutes. He decided to give the envelope an extra ten minutes before slicing it open. Insurance.

During the wait, he had considered possible ways of breaking free from the apartment building. The guards would be rough, but his unexpected speed and the strength of his bionics limbs might well counter them. Certainly one guard wouldn't be a problem. Getting both was still a question mark, and he hardly dared play with odds—however long in his favor—at such a time. If he were wrong the city of Atlanta, its inhabitants, surrounding suburbs and an area covering hundreds of miles downwind of the city could be called on to pay the ultimate price.

The guards stayed well apart. They were experts in their job, and he didn't for a moment underestimate their capabilities. What finally brought him to reject entirely the idea of taking them on, of chancing getting them both, was that it might accomplish exactly nothing. He knew enough of the workings of Franks' mind by now to know that the two guards were only the most immediate security against any violation by him of Franks' elaborately laid plans. Sam's security cross-hatching would unquestionably include guards in the building across the street. If anyone from the building with the bomb showed up *not* according to plan or notification, hell would literally break loose.

Steve didn't have to inspect the rear of his building to be sure that every doorway and window was boarded up and barred. The apartment told him that—with the exception of the door leading to the hallway, every door in the apartment, including those for the closets, had been removed. Steve was *always* in direct view of at least one of his guards, even when using the bathroom.

Sam had left nothing to chance.

Steve opened the letter.

Austin:

Sorry it's not the Hilton. You can expect to be stuck where you are for at least several days. At least now you know and can accommodate your routine to what you've got to do. I wouldn't have anyone else handle it.

First, let's cover any emergency situations—unplanned ones according to Murphy's laws of physics—such as fire, flood, electrical breakdown. No matter what happens, keep in mind you can't repeat can *not* use the phone for outgoing calls. Getting half your head blown away can ruin your whole day. However, in event things do come unglued, your watchdogs have several emergency numbers to call. There's a phone booth on the street corner two blocks east of your building. They each know what to do and who to call, and, more important, how to assure the authenticity of any call they might have to make.

Outside of fire or an airplane landing in your lap there's really no reason to leave the premises, which could be unhealthy. In case of fire, use the extinguishers you'll find in every room. Except for some catastrophe external to the building, the odds in your favor of being left alone are something like a hundred thousand to one. I repeat, that's in your favor. I thought you would feel better to know that number comes from a large and capable electronic brain.

I don't anticipate that anyone from this organization will see you at any time during the next several days to a week, until arrangements are made to bring you back to the airport. If we do need to visit you, be sure to accept such a visit only after you get full identification. The ID will be with my voice, either live or taped. You will hear, in this specific order, my full name, your full name, the names of the two spacecraft for your lunar mission, and, finally, the first, third, and fifth numbers of your blue suit

147

serial number. I realize this sounds melodramatic to you, but it is secure—which is what we're after. If anyone attempts entry without this preliminary, tell the guards to cut them down. And resist any temptation to play games. This handwritten letter has no copies—destroy yours—but the guards know the ID. If you try playing host to outsiders, they have their orders. I'm sure you understand the consequences not only to you but a whole city and its people.

I know you're not going to like what comes next, but it seemed the only safe way of handling this situation. Stay with me now, moon man. This gets a bit tricky.

The bomb activates exactly five hours after I last adjusted the mechanism, so it's just about coming to full life as you read this. When I eliminated that fifth interlock only one was left. I know that you're familiar with the hardware, but another go at it can't hurt.

The sixth interlock has been modified to accept an elimination command by VHF radio signal. Once the interlock goes there's no way to prevent the bomb from exploding.

But—and this is a very big but—I've added something to the hardware. When you finish this letter, look at the rear of the assembly and you'll find ten numbered buttons. They come alive every fifteen minutes. Shortly after you read this, you'll see a red light start to flash just above the panel of buttons. At the same time a warning tone will come on. It's a nasty screech.

Now, everything here is critical.

When the red light and the tone signal are activated, you have exactly five minutes in which to complete an action that puts the bomb back on interlock safety. In other words, when you see the flashing light and hear the signal that device is alive and counting down to detonation. You've got to stop that auto-sequence.

The way you do that is to depress three of the ten buttons. You depress them in a specific sequence—they are the same three numbers I'll use for identification in case we have to reach you directly.

The first, third, and fifth numbers of your USAF serial number.

If you depress these numbers properly you cancel out

the auto-sequence. If you fail to do so then I've lost one hell of a pilot. At the end of the five minutes that begins with the red flashing light and the tone signal, the bomb detonates.

There's no way to stop it.

If you punch the right numbers in wrong sequence, no damage done. A yellow light flashes. That's when you should take a deep breath and start over again.

If you punch the proper numbers in proper sequence, you win a cigar. The red light also goes out and the tone signal cuts off. A green light comes on and stays lit until the timer inside the bomb begins the new sequences and you get the red light and the tone signal again, fifteen minutes later.

I'm sure you'll be glad to know that there's a way to shut down the whole system and to renew all six interlocks, but it's better not to tell you how. Temptation is bad for the soul. That information will be provided to the American authorities when we confirm payment. It will be another numbered sequence.

Sorry to stick you in the middle like this, moon man, but you're the best I've got and the American government is likely to stay just a bit more on its toes because of your name.

Stay loose.

Sam

Steve made an instant decision and shouted at the watchdogs. One was by his side at once. Not the other. He stayed in the doorway with his automatic rifle pointed at both men.

Steve handed the letter to the man by his side. "Read this," he told him, "and be sure to read it carefully." The guard looked up at Steve, then turned to the other man.

"This isn't a game," Steve said harshly. "You read the letter one at a time." He went to a couch and sprawled across the cushions. "One of you can cover me while the other reads."

The first guard turned white as he went through the letter. Without a word he crossed the room, turned to face Steve with the weapon leveled at him, and handed the letter to his companion. Again Steve waited until he saw awareness grow in the face of the second man.

"Okay. You both know the rules," Steve said. "If at any time I seem to go ape, and you don't understand what I'm doing, for God's sake don't bother with me until I follow that insanity you've just read. Do you understand? Because if I mess up we're *all* gone. The time between punching those numbers doesn't let you get far enough away from that thing"—he pointed to the bomb—"to do you a bit of good. Being around an exploding hydrogen bomb can ruin your whole day."

The guards stared at one another. Not a word between them. They weren't being the strong silent types right now. They had just found out there was a nightmare going on and they were right in the middle of it.

Damn you, Sam ...

He let the anger rush through him. Maybe it would clear his head. And maybe it wouldn't make any difference. He didn't know, he couldn't really think. Being pinned to this building. Worse. If the intricate negotiations and payment of a billion dollars somehow fell apart, then Sam, or any of several people clued in to the details of the system, could detonate the hydrogen bomb *at any time.*

Just send off that VHF radio signal ...

Again he reviewed his immediate options. He could try to kill both guards. If he did, what then? He couldn't use the phone in the apartment. That rigged explosive charge. Which meant getting out of the building to the phone booth on the corner. To do that he had to kill both guards, quickly, run the gauntlet of whatever security teams Sam Franks had set up outside the building, find the booth in working order and—

Would he get through to McKay or Goldman in time? Because if he didn't ...

Even if he were to kill the guards and run for his own life—which he knew he could never do—it would be a waste of energy. No chance of getting far enough away to escape the fireball and the thermal yield and the punch of the shock wave and—

He cut off the thought. He was trapped. He had to stay with the bomb, play punch-the-buttons, hope negotiations went as planned and—

And what . . . ?"

So what if everything went exactly as Sam Franks and Jonathan Sperry and that miserable Kuto wanted? What then? Well, if Sam had told the absolute truth, and everything went perfectly, how could he be sure that Sam still wouldn't set off the bomb?

He didn't know.

He had no way of knowing what was happening or actually planned.

Or who might decide to send the radio signal.

Or when.

The red light began to flash.

CHAPTER 20

No one moved.

They stared at the terrible weapon that had suddenly come alive. Time for mental exercise was over.

The tone signal knifed into their ears, twisting and stabbing with its screech.

Move, Austin!

He went slowly to the bomb. He stared at it, the light almost hypnotic, the screech grinding through his teeth and his bones. The guards stared no longer at the bomb but at him. In that instant Steve had become their life.

He leaned forward, studying the numbers. His fingers moved to the panel.

Two.

He felt the sweat trickling down his face, the tremble starting in his muscles.

Nine.

He hesitated, the awful signal. Salt from his sweat now smarting in his eye. He shook his head.

Four.

The signal went out. Green. Steady.

Silence, broken only by the sound of one of his guards throwing up on the floor.

The moment he completed the numbered sequence they had fifteen minutes before the next sequence began with the light and the signal. And five minutes more before the thing would go off.

He found some relief in taunting the guards. "If we ever got out of here we'd waste a minute or two getting outside. What about the reception committee Franks is sure to have left across the street? Okay, forget about that. We get outside and what happens? We've got to get a vehicle. We're in the middle of a city. During the day the traffic would slow us. Night? If we could do sixty miles an hour —which we can't—we could put twenty miles between us and this *thing*." He gestured at the bomb. "It would be more like ten or twelve miles. And that's at least thirty-two million tons of explosive power there. No way, troops."

With no way out they resorted to the only thing they could do, which was to guard Steve Austin. They needed to keep him alive and well and on the premises to do his job. They also knew Sam Franks well enough to suspect that the numbered sequence stabbed out by Austin might be only one part of what had to be done.

The strain on Steve was mental and physical. There could be nothing more than snatches at sleep, and those were brief minutes of yielding to total exhaustion. When the tone screeched through the room he came violently awake, his subconscious howling at him to stay awake, to be alert, to stab his fingers into the numbers in the demanded sequence.

The bomb was more than a thing now. It was alive and

it was malignant. It was immediate death on an over-whelming scale, and it brooded malevolently, seeming to expand in size, to taunt them. The more hours that passed the more distant became the men with him. Steve recognized their entrapment with him and came to ignore them.

Nothing existed but the bomb and its obscene call for attention. Steve dragged the couch so that it stood just in front of the panel of numbers. When he slept it was with a guard standing nearby, always ready to prod him awake should his growing stupor take over.

Two days came and went.

His eye was, he knew, bloodshot. Even his hands had begun to shake. He held up his bionics arm in front of his face, studying it, turning the hand and flexing the steel fingers.

And the man-made miracle trembled, because not even steel and cabling and electronics and nuclear drive could overcome the connections to his shoulder stump, which led to his brain, which was profoundly weary. The effect of repetition was brutal. A sense of suffocating weight drove against him. He wandered from vague introspection to towering rage.

And all the while he punched buttons and stared at the panel and the green light that wavered in front of his eye now as the flashing red faded away, except for the glow burned into his retina, and the screech echoed forever, leaving and coming back, ringing through the farthest reaches of his exhausted, aching mind.

Again.

Sitting with his elbows on his knees, his head weighing a ton, his throat dry, his tongue swollen, his back twisted and agonizing. He slept this way, a near-zombie permitted faint escape in stolen moments of sleep before being whipped back to the fading reality of the present.

He was worshipper, servant, priest and sacrificial lamb before this ultimate thermonuclear god.

The bomb had become truly alive to him. Gone from his consciousness was the recollection that this was a machine, a mass of steel and uranium and deuterium and plastic and gold cones and explosive lenses. The innards of the Thing had taken on sentience, they throbbed and

153

hummed and life coursed through their cables and wires.

And Steve groped at the altar, and pressed the buttons to please It.

What drove Steve near to a special sort of madness was that he didn't *know* if the sequence of numbers he punched again and again really did the slightest bit of good.

Would the bomb really detonate if he failed to punch the numbers on command of the screeching sound and the blinking red light? How could he know this for *certain?*

Was it possible he was victim to a monstrous perversion concocted by the twisted humor of Sam Franks?

He didn't know and he couldn't know, and he couldn't do anything except follow the instructions Franks had used to chain him to the bomb. *Because—*

Because Butukama had been real.

And so had the nuclear flash that destroyed the *Dorina.*

Even during the brief interludes of sleep, he dreamed. He kept seeing that awful fireball—in the middle of the night, a terrible lash of a star gutting a city, the heat flash stabbing out a hundred miles in every direction, the fireball erupting to miles above the city, mottled and horrible, crushing and grinding, spawning the shock waves, tons of radioactive earth hurled out in every direction.

He would shake the vision from his mind. In that escape he would be back in Apollo, rushing away from the earth, climbing up an invisible line, farther and farther from Hell, bathing himself in the sweet nothingness of space.

A quarter of a million miles gone from It, and he would look back on the blue-and-white marble rolling through the velvety blackness of space, a half-earth suspended against infinity. And on the dark side, beyond that thin reddish line, a spark would appear. A single pinpoint of light, brighter than the sun and the stars, a light to prick the balloon of darkness, flaring swiftly. The entire globe began to burn—and he came bursting from the dream, soaked in perspiration . . .

Three days.

Four.

Groggy, mouth dry, once more he forced himself to turn, to face It.

But there was something else . . . He fought to clear his head, felt the beard on his face. He turned.

The guards stood in front of him, one close, the other across the room, automatic weapons pointed at him.

He tried to understand . . . there was something else in the room . . . standing on the other side from the bomb. Who—? Familiar. A woman . . . He'd seen her before . . . ?

She was holding a gun on him.

Voice. She was talking *and he knew her voice.*

"Bring in a chair from the kitchen." Of course he knew it, but not like this. Before it had been . . . ? Still couldn't remember.

"Get in the chair, Steve."

He shook his head. There it was. Right on time . . . right on the old button. The flashing light and the screech signal. Giddy with weariness, he stabbed buttons.

Yellow.

Yellow? Yellow is wrong. Do it again. Stab.

Good old green light.

The fog went away as he was jerked roughly from the couch onto the straight-backed chair. Immediately rope coiled about his arms and chest and—

Not rope, thin cable in a plastic liner. What was going on? Cable around his arms and legs. He couldn't move.

She motioned with the gun in her hand. "Be sure," she ordered the guard next to him. "Check the binding." The guard leaned down behind him.

Hissing noise.

He stared. The woman had barely moved the gun but had squeezed the trigger several times. No explosive charge. That hiss. He knew the weapon. Compressed-air needle gun, spring backup, holding ninety frangible needles each filled with a poisonous derivative of nerve gas. You added the poison from a scolopendra or some other type of tropical centipede to the nerve poison. The effect of scolopendra—immobilizing pain. Shock so great you can't control your body. In the time it takes to fight the agony the nerve-gas poison does its work. Takes maybe

155

ten, fifteen seconds to die, but from the instant the frangible needle explodes within the body a person's totally helpless.

The guard threw out his arms in violent reaction to the needle darts entering his body. Moments later, the second guard, reacting with the instinct of his years of training and experience, was spinning around, weapon in his hands. He needn't have bothered. He took one needle in the face, another in the neck, several in his chest and stomach. His body twisted in agony. He collapsed to the floor. It was over.

The woman turned back to Steve, replacing the weapon in her purse. She walked toward him. Finally it was beginning to get through.

He stared, not believing. The sound of her voice . . . but that perfume . . .

The perfume. That woman in his room who'd tried to kill him. It was the same.

But she had a different voice. One he was sure he knew. "Oleg. Mikhail Oleg!"

CHAPTER 21

"Michèle," she said in a voice very different from the one he'd just heard. "Michèle when I'm myself."

The voice changed. "And when it is necessary to be Mikhail"—she shrugged, smiled—"You seem surprised, Colonel."

"Hardly the word for it."

"You also look a mess."

"Lousy room service. By the way, how'd you get in?"

"You seem to forget, Colonel, that I'm also Oleg, a very important part of this operation. Naturally I was able to discover and use Franks' ID. The guards have seen me before, except at such times I went by the name Yvette Rochelle—a much safer courier for my government than the infamous Mikhail Oleg—so well known to Pentronics and presumably a missing traitor to my own country."

"You really are a woman?"

"I should hope so." And in that moment whatever male mannerisms he remembered of Mikhail were entirely gone. Only Michèle (alias Yvette) remained. Of course. That night in his room. Enough light, just enough to see the woman she wanted him to see.

"You are no doubt also wondering, Colonel, how I managed the masquerade for so long within a world of men?"

"That thought was crossing my mind."

"There is little time. But for a man with your remarkable number of lives, nothing should be a surprise. Actually, it was rarely a problem. To be properly cautious I took chemical injections to produce a light beard and suppress the uniquely feminine attributes. The voice was a simple matter of training. And the luxurious life-style affording so much privacy that Pentronics specializes in took care of the rest. Fortunately one was not obliged to use communal facilities, and—as you may have noticed—I have made a point of being something of a recluse."

No wonder they could never get a handle on who was trying to kill him. If they trapped a woman, Mikhail Oleg was always able to appear suddenly on the scene, and who the hell was going to doubt him?

But this was something else. "For a woman," he said remembering her in that MIG-21 fighter, "you're one hell of a pilot."

Found a nerve there, he thought, watching her face.

"Colonel Austin, for you to discriminate between male and female where flying is concerned, well, you disappoint me. And if you're wondering why my government sent a woman to do what you assume to be a man's job, the explanation is simple. Not only could I play different roles with less risk of detection. I also happened to be the best man"—she almost smiled—"trained and available for the job."

"Like you say, Michèle, or whatever your name is, you're obviously very good. I don't think Sam ever has suspected the Russian government was on to him. Especially that they had a plant right in the front office."

She moved a chair in front of him. "Which is our next topic, Colonel. I have questions to ask you. You will provide the answers. Would you please strain against your bonds to break loose?"

"What?"

"Go ahead, Austin. The sooner you're aware that you are bound with cable and that breaking loose is impossible, the sooner we will get our matters settled."

Cable, all right. He strained, twisted. Just enough. Then he slumped.

"How long have Sam Franks and Pentronics been working for the American government?" She was obviously fishing.

"You know the man longer than I do. You know he wasn't working for—"

"*Please,* Colonel."

"But you said you believed Sam was working for the American government. That's ridiculous. If they ever get their hands on him they'll—"

"Austin, we are wasting time and words. You know what we learned of your friend Schiller and his connection with the CIA. We have reason to believe there's much more to your relationship with OSO than we can prove. We know you have spent time with a man by the name of Oscar Goldman. And Goldman is the right arm of Jackson McKay. Certain things are obvious. We are convinced you were sent by your government to bring Sam Franks back into service. And the entire Pentronics organization with him. And very convenient that would be for the American government."

"Convenient?"

"Pentronics is well know to certain political leaders, to governments, to industrial groups. It is a lethal power, dangerous in its own right. But most important is that it is *known.* With Sam Franks working again for the American government, Pentronics becomes a most valuable instrument for the United States. With the scars of Vietnam so deep in your people, they would hardly agree to any more similar wars. Yet the United States *must* interfere in the affairs of other governments. I admit it's an excellent arrangement. Pentronics is recognized for what it is—an international paramilitary organization. But with a key operative in your employ, it can do things for the U.S. it wouldn't dare do itself. And without fingers being pointed. What we do not know, however, is *if* and *when* you succeeded in your mission—"

"Oleg, for God's sake," he broke in, "if all this were true, then what the hell am I doing playing nursemaid to this damned bomb?" He nodded toward the metal case in the room. "That thing is real. You must believe that. It's thirty-two megatons waiting to go off, and if we were playing games with Franks I sure as hell wouldn't be *here*."

She studied him for a moment before speaking. "There are ways to—"

Screech.

The signal knifed through her words, froze her where she stood. She moved around the bomb and stared at the flashing red light, then turned to Steve bound to his chair.

"How much time is there?"

"Here's your chance, Oleg, to go out in a blaze of glory."

The needle gun almost leaped into her hand.

Steve laughed. "Just what are you going to do with that thing? Go ahead, pull the trigger. You'll be there with me soon enough."

The gun was slowly returned to her purse. "I do not think so. If the bomb goes off, then this city dies. And everyone with it. I will wait."

"Checkmate," he said. Since he was immobilized, he had to give her the numbered sequence or risk blowing up Atlanta. "The numbers. Two, nine, four. In that sequence. Don't get excited. You'd never get away in time."

She moved to the panel and punched the buttons. The tone went silent and the steady green light came on. "When does it happen again?"

"Fifteen minutes."

"It is enough." She went quickly to the large footlocker with the tools and electrical equipment. He watched her in silence, glad he'd given no demonstration of his true strength. Not even the cables could hold him, he felt sure, but any struggle on his part to break free could hardly be successful before poisoned darts would be pumping into his body. And now that she had the numbered code for the bomb, to prevent detonation, she had no need to keep him alive—except for whatever information she felt she still had to get from him. At least there was no hope for her to punch the numbers on the bomb panel and still have enough time to escape. Twenty minutes would barely be sufficient and—

Unless she had a helicopter ready close by—

He cursed himself. She *could* have bought all the time she needed. And if she did have a chopper standing by then she could get from him what she needed, and leave in plenty of time to escape even the thermonuclear lash of that unholy device in the room with them.

It struck him that his strength, God-given or man-created through his bionics systems, was of no real use to him. Michèle Oleg was something. She had managed to outwit Sam Franks and Jonathan Sperry *and* Hiroshi Kuto. Not to mention himself. She was a superb undercover agent, a practiced mime, a fighter pilot and, he was reasonably sure, had equal skills in electronics, weapons and God knew what else. He also had first-hand knowledge that she was a killer, and the only thing keeping him alive at this moment was that she believed she needed information from him more than she needed him dead.

Which, he knew, was a short-lived situation.

She knelt in front of him. With deft movement she stripped the ends off two electrical wires, secured the open wire to small alligator clips. The other end of the wire she connected to an electrical plug. Not a word was spoken by her. Steve remained silent, all too aware of what she intended. She busied herself for ten minutes, glancing occasionally at her watch. She was waiting when the tone signal and red light activated. She hit the buttons in sequence. Green shone steady.

160

She stood, holding the wire end with the clips. "Is this going to be necessary?" Her voice was flat. He looked away.

A knife in her hand, she bent, slashed away a trousers leg, tossed aside the fabric. One glance at his face and the knife swung.

He felt the sharp, stabbing sensation of bionics-related pain. He looked down. Oleg had slashed deep into the plastiskin of his right leg. She cut again, tearing away the plastiskin to expose the intricate systems.

The alligator clips went into the leg, were fastened to the bionics nerves. She went across the room. He strained to keep control.

She plugged in the other end of the wire.

A savage jolt went through his body, exploded in his brain. He had no control, no knowledge of what he was going to do. His body trembled violently.

My God! The pain . . . impossible . . . I never knew . . .

She removed the plug and he gasped for air, on the edge of uncontrollable muscle spasms.

Before he could think she plugged in again. His body writhed with agony searing his brain. He felt his muscles standing rigid as steel. His heart pounded and he knew not much more could kill him.

A third time she plugged in again. Through the horror he tried to think.

"Enough!" he gasped, slumping in the chair. He could hardly breathe, fought for self-control, gasping. His tongue protruded and he tried to bring it back. He closed his eyelids, trying to calm himself.

She knew her business. Nothing personal, of course.

"Is it enough?" He opened his eyes. She sat before him, legs crossed. He nodded quickly, the picture of a man who can't take any more. And it wasn't an act.

"Are you recruiting Franks for your government? Also Pentronics?"

"Yes."

"And you, Colonel Austin? It is so much easier this way, don't you agree?"

He nodded.

"To whom do you report?"

"Same office."

"Be specific, Colonel. I'd hate to—"

"OSO," he said quickly.

"I thought so. It really is McKay, again."

He nodded, watching her glance again at her watch. She sat quietly for a minute, and he was grateful for the reprieve. He felt his strength coming back, and he knew no matter what he must not let that wire be plugged in again. The minute passed and the tone signal stabbed into his ears.

Already? Where did the time go—

She pushed the buttons and returned to the seat in front of him. "We are off to a good start," she said. "How do you report?"

"Telephone, if safe. Or in person, if possible."

"Have you been in touch with OSO lately?"

He shook his head. "No chance."

"The number, please."

He told her the OSO office number.

"Not that one. That is in the confidential phone directory. Everyone has that. I hope we will not need—"

"*No*. I didn't know what you meant. It's 858-6421. That's the direct line for McKay."

"You are certain?"

"I'm sure. Look, if you don't believe me why don't you—"

"When I dial that number, if it is *not* the private line to McKay . . ." She looked at the wire still clamped to his bionics leg.

"I *swear* it's the number . . ."

Disgust showed on her face. "If there is one thing I cannot tolerate, Austin, it's a coward!"

"Please. It's the truth!"

She rose to her feet.

That's it, Michèle. Just go to that telephone. Make that call. Make it . . .

He would crawl or kiss her feet so long as she went to that phone and—

She stopped and turned to him. "In just over one hour and ten minutes from now this bomb will explode. There will be no stopping it. Certainly you will be in no position to do so. Even if I wished to stop the explosion it is beyond my control. The radio signal to detonate the bomb will be sent automatically. No one need be there. We will have no more than another ten minutes together and then you will have another hour by yourself before it is over." She glanced at the phone. "But if you have been lying to me you will, as you now understand, spend a most unpleasant last hour."

"Just *call!*"

She went to the phone and lifted the receiver. Slowly, holding the telephone to her ear, ready not to miss a single click or sound, she dialed the Washington area code and started the number.

He felt the sweat down his neck as the sounds of the telephone dial seemed to fill the room.

Five digits.

Six.

The dial came around on the seventh number.

The explosion went through the room. Something warm and moist was across his face. Ears hammering from the blast, he opened his eyes.

She was still upright, and he watched, stared, as her body collapsed to the floor.

For a long moment it all seemed to be happening in slow motion. His mind was partly there, in the room, but he also had a phantom view of a silvery MIG-21 rolling gracefully against a deep blue sky, and there was this strange, unbidden sense of loss—

The feeling was abruptly gone as he felt something warm trickling down his face, and he knew it was *her*— not his—blood. He looked at the form on the floor. Reality pounded back at him.

Sam had finally done him a favor . . .

And now what, he thought. Little more than an hour before the bomb went off. If the negotiations didn't work out as Sam planned. And if Oleg was right, the bomb was set to go anyway. Who to believe? Steve didn't know, but he did know he'd better work on the most dismal premise —which was . . .

163

Little more than an hour to go before the bomb went off—*provided he still kept pushing the right buttons.*

The tone signal stabbed at him.

Five minutes.

CHAPTER 22

The sound galvanized him into action. He took deep breaths, balanced himself as well as he could, and began to strain. He felt the cables pressing deeply into his arms, one human and one bionic.

Another deep breath, and a tremendous effort to snap the cables or break them free from their knots.

He gasped with the sudden pain.

It wasn't working.

The realization stunned him. Then he understood. The left arm had ten times the strength of his right. But when he strained his arms and the bionics limb exerted its pressure, the right arm couldn't stand the biting effect of the cable. Well before the cable snapped it would cut open his flesh and tear apart the arm itself.

Your legs ... Use your legs.

Of course. He braced carefully, and strained.

The cable seemed to stretch. But only barely. He tried again, this time thrusting with his legs—side to side, back and forth.

The cables held.

Time was rushing away. *He couldn't break the cables. Not enough power left in that leg where she'd cut it open.* He glanced down at the wire still leading from his bionics limb where she'd slashed it naked. He'd try both feet on the floor, get the weight on the balls of the feet.

He almost cried out. The feedback from his slashed bionics leg was being interpreted by his natural system as a mutilated part of itself and danger signals—pain—were building up rapidly inside him.

He threw everything into downward pressure, trying to jump. The mangled leg gave him only partial performance, but the left leg was strong as ever.

He left the floor in a ludicrous hop-and-jump and twisted his body wildly as he felt the upward movement.

When he came down it was at a crazy angle. But it was working.

One chair leg came down with a splintering crack.

It split, then broke.

His right leg was still clamped rigidly.

But not the left. He'd do it again.

He braced himself. Balance. That was everything.

All the weight was now on the left leg. This was the one that counted.

Again that ridiculous lunge off the floor. He came down with a jarring crash. More wood splintered. He was on his side and kicked wildly. Wood broke into pieces.

The cable was loose now.

Staggering, he made it to his feet. But his arms were still bound. Had the cables loosened? Barely. He could move his fingers. It would have to do.

He stumbled to the bomb, stared at the flashing red light. He'd forgotten all about the screeching sound that had gouged into his brain all these hours. He looked at the numbers. They were set up in the manner of a touch-dial telephone:

1	2	3
4	5	6
7	8	9
	0	

He turned his back, tried to lean backward so his fingers could reach the numbers. Remember, he told himself, it's all reverse now. He groped, his right arm numb. One number; the second; the third.

He turned around.

The yellow light was on.

Three times his fingers groped, pushed.

The tone signal. Yellow light stared at him as he turned. He refused to think. Turn.

Feel the numbers.

Two.

Down to the bottom. That single number.

Nine.

One more, one more . . .

There's the first row. Now the second. There . . .

Four.

Silence.

The relief almost gagged him. He sucked in air, told himself to be careful, not to hyperventilate. To take it slow, easy. Fifteen minutes before the next sequence . . .

It took him five more minutes to wriggle free from the cables around his arms. Everything revolved around the fact that if it was to happen, a VHF signal would be used to detonate the bomb. Well, he'd handled enough nukes to disarm the thing. He'd done that before and—

Don't.

There were built-in safeties that set off an internal explosive charge to wreck the bomb if someone tampered with it. He needed special tools. And if he knew Sam Franks, that normal disarm mechanism would do just the opposite of what anyone planned. It would most likely set off the nuclear weapon itself.

What to do? Punching numbers every fifteen minutes was a career that soon wouldn't have any meaning to it. At the least, failure to immobilize the device would leave Sam's enormous blackmail ploy intact.

Somehow he had to block that radio signal. There was no other way.

Back to basics. He forced himself to think calmly. What he had to do was to attenuate the signal. To damp it out so completely that the VHF signal, or even a UHF signal, couldn't get through to the bomb.

Remember: an antenna does not receive signals. It's a passive device. Signals are sent to it. An antenna is a dumb creature. If you put it under the ground it doesn't work well. Why? You're attenuating the signal and it can't get through to that dumb, waiting antenna.

Well, he couldn't get the bomb below the ground. And the antenna was built in as an integral part of the bomb casing. His problem would have to be solved right where he was.

Okay, next. The next best thing was to cover the antenna with any conducting material that could be placed at ground potential, in other words, ground it.

The VHF/UHF signal is a tight frequency. It does not penetrate the earth. Or water.

Water?

Oh, God . . . Of course!

Sam had said they could be in the house a week. Even two weeks. Sam was a planner, a stickler for detail. He had the kitchen stocked. *Well* stocked. Which wouldn't mean just food and liquids.

He dragged his way into the kitchen, tearing open cupboards. There . . . beautiful. Nothing like being efficient.

Three rolls of aluminum foil. He brought the packages back into the living room. He stopped for a moment, dropped the packages. He had to get the bomb into the bathroom. But the thing weighed some two hundred pounds. With that leg . . . what did he do now? He'd try. He'd better . . .

It was shove and push and strain. He went back to the tool locker. A long plumber's wrench. It would do. He managed to lift the bomb sufficiently to get the long wrench beneath. That gave him leverage. It took nearly ten minutes but by then he had the bomb in the bathroom.

The red light.

That signal.

The buttons.

Less than forty-five minutes.

He had to get the bomb into the bathtub.

He went to his knees, his right leg jerking spasmodically as he began to apply pressure. The wrench let him get his

167

finger underneath. The side of the bomb was against the smooth facing of the tub.

Pain moved through his thigh and into his hip.

Move.

He got his left arm under the bomb. He used his human arm for balance. He heaved with all his strength. The huge case came up, balanced on the edge of the tub. He slid it down with a crash.

He slumped over, breathing hard, elated.

Kiss the back of your hand later, Austin. For God's sake . . .

He went to the living room, and dragged the aluminum foil back with him. It was a backbreaking job getting underneath the bomb but that wrench again gave him leverage. He wrapped every part of the bomb with the aluminum foil, leaving a flap open until the red light and the tone signal activated.

The re-sequencing at worst had to go through at least two more cycles before the radio signal to detonate the bomb would be sent. From that point on—if he were still alive—he would have to keep re-sequencing with the hope that as long as he did the radio signal might not work. Oleg had told him when the detonation signal would be sent. Maybe Sam's blackmail would work and he wouldn't send it. In any case, he had to take advantage of every second he had to try to insulate the bomb from the signal.

Timing.

He returned with several long electric wires. He busied himself with splicing new alligator clips to one wire. The other end he stripped down to the copper, braiding the copper into a single section about two inches in length.

The light and tone signal again. He punched buttons.

Only one more time . . . ?

He closed off the tub drain and turned the faucet on full. Water poured into the tub, filling rapidly.

He cursed himself for sloppy thinking and rushed to the kitchen. He returned to the bathroom with a large box of table salt. He tore open the top and dumped the contents into the tub, sloshing it around. The salt greatly improved the characteristics of the water as a conductor. The water

168

was electrically connected to the plumbing system the moment he activated his makeshift shield.

Everything else was ready. He had the alligator clips of the wire clamped to two sides of the aluminum foil wrapping that covered the bomb.

The signal.

He pushed the buttons, crushed the open flap of tinfoil over the sequencing panel. He almost literally threw himself across the room, stabbed the open end of the wire into the third pin of the socket in the wall.

Ordinary socket. Three pins; three openings. Only top two normally used. The bottom opening, circular, used by power company for grounding household circuits. He jammed the open wire into that opening.

He went back to the tub. The faucets on again, full blast. Moments later the bomb was completely immersed in salt water.

If he remembered correctly, the antenna in the bomb casing was now blanked off from any outside signal, especially from a distance. In effect, that antenna was now "beneath the ground."

If everything had worked out in his makeshift system, the antenna would no longer be able to function as a proper receiver for an outside signal.

If he was wrong, he likely would never know it. Nor would anyone else in the city of Atlanta.

He kept on working. You don't rest on shaky laurels.

He needed to try at double insurance. He looked at his watch. Two minutes down, thirteen to go. If he was still there reading his watch when the sweep hand went past thirteen minutes, he'd have good reason to believe the thing was working.

To the living room. The television set that had never been turned on. He found a long extension cord, plugged it into a socket, connected the TV cord to that, then dragged the set into the bathroom. He heaved it to the toilet seat, as close as he could get the set to the bomb in the tub.

What he now needed was to generate a strong interfering radio signal in the room—a signal much like the broad spectrum of lightning. Between destroying the effectiveness of the antenna with his jury-rigged bathtub system, *and* generating a strong interference signal, he might save an entire city that for all he knew had not submitted to Sam Franks' blackmail threat, had not perhaps believed the reality of the threat, despite Sam's elaborate attempts to make it convincing. Or a city that was doomed in any case, according to Oleg, unless he was successful.

He studied the protective covering along the back of the TV set. When the covering was removed normally it cut off all current to the set. The average householder who messed with a set was playing with nearly 20,000 volts. Steve needed to get that covering off without stopping the household current into the set.

He reached out, stabbed with a stiff forefinger of his bionics hand. It pierced the thin covering. When he was through he had an opening large enough for what he needed to do. He turned on the set. It was hot, still receiving current.

He turned off the set. On the side of the picture tube was a high voltage lead; a heavy cable similar to the type found in automobile ignition systems. He picked up a roll of electrical tape. He took a moment out to study the set, then pulled the high voltage lead from the set.

Now the tape to secure this lead to a position about an inch away from the anode connection of the tube.

He went back to the tool chest, found a heavy marking pencil. With the pencil he traced a graphite line from the lead's end to the anode connector.

He turned on the set.

A thin, crackling spark, a writhing filament of blue flame leaped from the lead to the anode. What had been graphite was now instantly carbon. The thin blue flame was a thing of joy for him to see . . . a tiny flickering tongue of lightning that was constantly generating a broad spectrum radio signal.

Which had to interfere with any other signal being sent to the bomb.

He fell back against the bathroom wall and stared at his watch. Twenty seconds.

CHAPTER 23

The sweep second-hand moved along the face of his watch.

He began to count down the final seconds.

It didn't work.

He was numb. Drained. The watch's face blurred.

He waited passively to focus again. He knew he should make a special effort. No use. He was done.

His watch came into focus.

Forty-five seconds *past* the thirteen minutes.

It still wasn't over. He didn't know how long the detonation signal would be broadcast. If the system had been set for blind automatic as Oleg indicated, then they would use a backup. Wherever they had the transmitter it was likely plugged into an electrical outlet for power. But they'd know something could go wrong in such an arrangement, so they'd probably set up for local power with a nickel-cadmium backup. You got enough juice that way to transmit the signal for hours. Or for days, if you stacked enough batteries with the transmitter. He just didn't know, but he did believe he had no choice except to assume the signal might be transmitted for some unspecified period of time.

By now Sam, or whoever was sending that signal, would know something had gone wrong. He wondered about Sam. Oleg appearing on the scene could mean that the others had decided Sam's intention to keep a bargain was not to their liking. Whatever his twisted thinking, Sam probably meant to stick by the terms of his offered deal—however monstrous and terrifying they might be.

Well, the immediate need was to get another kind of attention. He dragged himself to his feet, felt his energy slowly returning. No sense of triumph, just relief. He stood, rocky, controlling his breathing before moving.

His first step sent him crashing against the wall. His leg. The circuits were going? For the first time he noticed the spasms rippling the plastiskin. He could feel again. It wasn't pleasant. He worried that the whole bionics system might soon go out. He could end up unconscious on the floor.

He kept the right leg as stiff as possible, walking clumsily through the apartment. He went to the shattered body of Michèle Oleg. The gun. He tucked it in his belt.

Then to the guards. One submachine gun against a wall where he could reach it easily. He picked up the second gun and turned off the lights in the apartment. He walked slowly, dragging the stiff leg behind him, to the window. Kneeling on his good leg, keeping to the side of the window, he eased apart the heavy drapes and looked outside.

Night. He didn't even know.

A street lamp a hundred feet to his left. Near the lamp an appliance store. He used the muzzle of the gun to break the window. He fired a long burst, sweeping from left to right. The bullets tore into the plate glass of the store, sending glass crashing to the sidewalk. Almost at the same instant a burglar alarm clanged. Good. A cab without passengers moved into his line of sight. Steve squeezed off two short bursts. The slugs ripped the back of the cab, which took off in a rush.

He was back in the apartment, sitting on the floor with his back to the wall, the second submachine gun cradled in his arms, when the police broke down the front door. He held the gun extended from him as they came up the stairway, their own weapons at the ready. They disarmed him before they spoke a word, then stared at the three bodies sprawled about the room.

"Whatever you do," Steve told them, "don't touch anything in the bathroom." One policeman was staring at the bathtub and the TV set with its crackling blue flame.

He turned to Steve. "Is that thing in there what I think it is?"

"Are you on search alert?" Steve asked.

"Mister, just who the hell are you?" the officer demanded.

"Austin. Colonel Steve Austin.

"My God, it *is* you. I recognize you. We've been turning the city upside down looking for—"

"Officer, there's thirty-two million tons of real hell in that bathtub. I repeat, don't let anyone touch anything. Now, I got some numbers for you to call. *Fast.*"

The military had been standing by at key bases throughout the country, waiting, barely daring to hope. The Pentagon knew a bomb had been placed in the country. They didn't know *where*. They had to suspect there were several bombs.

The prime sites included cities such as Washington, D.C., New York, Chicago, Miami, St. Louis, San Francisco, Los Angeles, Seattle, Atlanta, New Orleans, Houston, Portland—major population centers. They'd been told a ship in the San Francisco Bay area held a backup device ready to go if they failed to cooperate.

Atlanta was only one of the prime suspects. And Atlanta, like the other possible targets, was covered by special bomb teams, all of which were on immediate standby.

Dobbins Air Force Base, at Marietta, had helicopter teams ready. Sixteen minutes after a white-faced policeman rushed to his car and reported by radio, Steve heard the pounding of rotor blades. Jolly Green Giants; he recognized them by their sound.

"They're landing two blocks away," he was told.

A special team. They'd worked for years with nukes. Disarming atomic and hydrogen bombs was their specialty. They talked with Steve for ten minutes before they went near the bomb. Then they brought in a mass of special gear. Minutes later the entire building was surrounded by an intense electromagnetic shield. Nothing was getting through that.

Steve didn't care any more. It was out of his hands. Finally.

He hardly knew what was happening when a medical team came from a second chopper. Morphine in his arm. Other attentions. He didn't know, didn't care.

He was unconscious before they took him to the Jolly Green and set off for the hospital at the airbase.

They let him sleep only six hours. Enough, they decided, to get back his strength. While he was out, the special team from the bionics laboratory in Colorado arrived.

Dr. Rudy Wells and Art Fanier at once went to work on him. Fanier was the man who'd created the bionics systems and trained Steve in their use. He couldn't repair anything in the hospital. He didn't need to yet. He disconnected the terminal endings to the leg. The rest would be done back at the secret facilities on The Rock.

"They've got to talk with you," Rudy Wells told Steve.

"I know. And one will get you ten Goldman's pacing the corridor outside. Better let him in before he has a stroke."

He quickly told Oscar Goldman everything he could remember at the moment. Enough to give a broad picture, to supply names and places. Goldman was recording it all while Steve laid it out. More than recording, really. It was being sent by telephone and radio to key military and government stations throughout the country, as well as to overseas bases.

Steve had been talking for nearly an hour when Dr. Wells rebelled and forced a halt. A needle. This time he slept for seventeen hours.

"I'm flattered," Steve said. "Not often the buddha comes out of his temple."

Which was true. Jackson McKay had flown to the laboratory in Colorado to speak personally with Steve Austin.

"Never mind," McKay said, "I won't be here long. Better things to do than babysit a hero with tin legs."

Steve grinned. "Still bubbling over with affection."

"We got Sperry," McKay told him.

"Go on."

"Kuto's on a tanker. Boxed in. Three B-52s overhead. We'll board the ship in a few hours."

Steve waited.

"Other governments are working with us. We've occupied Oristano and seven other major centers. We think there's more."

"Sam Franks?"

"Good or bad news, depending on your point of view. He's dead."

Steve didn't answer, didn't believe it. The man had outsmarted NATO, the top military and intelligence people in the world. God knew he'd gone sour, committed horrible atrocities—including killing his friend Marty Schiller. Still, it was hard to believe. Steve wondered if his information helped track Sam down; if he was responsible for his death. In a way he hoped so, and yet . . .

They must have given him something else, because the memory of Franks drifted out of his mind. Which was a relief.

But even as he went under, he knew it would be back. You just didn't dismiss Sam Franks that easy. . . .